THE ANGRY PLANET

Living creatures—individuals—Martians!

THE
ANGRY PLANET

AN AUTHENTIC FIRST-HAND ACCOUNT OF A JOUR-
NEY TO MARS IN THE SPACE-SHIP *Albatross*,
COMPILED FROM NOTES AND RECORDS BY
VARIOUS MEMBERS OF THE EXPEDITION,
AND NOW ASSEMBLED AND EDITED FOR
PUBLICATION BY

JOHN KEIR CROSS

FROM MANUSCRIPTS MADE AVAILABLE BY

Stephen MacFarlane

THE ILLUSTRATIONS ARE BY

Robin Jacques

COWARD-McCANN INC
NEW YORK

Typography by Robert Josephy

MANUFACTURED IN THE UNITED STATES OF AMERICA

TO AUDREY

THE STORY

The Story

IMPORTANT

Editor's Note on the Illustrations

Originally we had meant to illustrate this book with real photographs—Dr. McGillivray took several good cameras to Mars with him. He, Mr. MacFarlane, and the children, all used a lot of film in snapping the Martians, their houses, cities, landscapes, and so on. But there must have been something in the chemical composition of the rarefied air on Mars that was deleterious to the emulsion on the negatives, for when the photographs were developed on earth after the journey, we found that they were either completely blank or so misty that any reproduction of them was out of the question. However, Mr. Robin Jacques, the artist who has done all the drawings in this book, worked most carefully from descriptions supplied by the Albatross travelers. And they all agree that his pictures are true representations of what they saw during their fantastic adventures in the strange, romantic and terrible places they visited so many millions of miles away.   J.K.C.

Full Page Illustrations

THE ANGRY PLANET

CHAPTER I. AN INTRODUCTION BY STEPHEN MacFARLANE

MOST of the civilized world knows by this time the main outline of the story of the remarkable flight to the planet Mars made by Dr. McGillivray, of Aberdeen, Scotland, in his space-ship *Albatross*. This book, however, is the first publication to put forth any sort of description of the extraordinary adventures that befell Dr. McGillivray's party on what has been called "the Angry Planet." Naturally, Dr. McGillivray has published various articles in the scientific journals (he is now engaged on the compilation of a full-length book that will describe in detail his innumerable valuable findings). But he—being a scientist (and I know he will not mind my saying this)—is inclined in his works to pay little attention to what may be called the *human* side of things. So we have put together this book. It ignores—or at any rate only covers sketchily—the scientific aspect of the adventure, and concerns itself almost entirely with what happened before and during the flight, and on Mars itself.

Students of the Press will remember the world-wide sensation caused by the news, after Dr. McGillivray's return to earth, that there had been three stowaways on the *Albatross* during its visit to Mars—two boys and a girl. The Doctor's daring achievement in bridging some 35 million miles of space was spectacular enough, heaven knows: but to think that three young people—schoolchildren—had gone through the unique experience with him, and he had not even known of their presence in the *Albatross* till the space-ship was well away from the earth—that was news indeed! The children were fêted, filmed, interviewed, asked to speak on the radio, and presented to every Lord Mayor in the country (or so it seemed to them). By this time the shouting and the tumult have died a little, which is a good thing, for the children were heartily sick of all the fuss and were glad to get back to normal. Not that things in their own minds ever got out of perspective—they were, all three of them, too sensible to get swollen heads over the affair. But after their fantastic adventures on Mars they needed a rest in which to collect their thoughts. They have now had that rest—and, in one sense, this book proves that they have collected their thoughts; for, as you will see, they—the children—have helped to write it.

Perhaps I should, at this point, introduce myself. My name is Stephen MacFarlane, and I am (as perhaps some of you may know) a writer. I am also the uncle of one of the adventurous children—the youngest one, Mike Malone. The other two were (and, of course, still are) his cousins, Paul and Jacqueline Adam. Being Mike's cousins they are, in a sense, also related to me, although so distantly that we have never bothered to work it all out properly. They call me Uncle Steve, of course, but I like to think that this is mainly because uncle is a term of affection!

When Dr. McGillivray—my very good friend—began experimenting some years ago with rockets and spaceships, I was his only confidant. He is, as is well known, a reticent man, wrapped up in his scientific studies. His Doctor's degree comes from his having graduated in Philosophy at the University of St. Andrews. He is still quite a young man—in his early forties. But, as I have said, he was shy to a degree of disclosing any of his thoughts to outsiders—I was his only real friend. The history of our friendship is an interesting one, which, alas, I have no time to tell here. It will be sufficient to say that I valued his confidence deeply. When he told me that he was experimenting with rockets, that he believed strongly that he would some day design one capable of carrying passengers on stratosphere flights—that he even visualized rocket flights to the moon and the planets as a possibility, I was enormously excited. It was a subject I was intensely interested in myself. I had always believed in the possibility of life on other planets—life different from life as we knew it, perhaps, but still life. So I encouraged the Doctor with my enthusiasm, and even made over most

3

of my savings to him so that he could go on with his experiments.

That was our chief trouble—money. The cost of the experiments was prodigious. It was a matter, you see—putting it briefly—of finding a fuel. The designing of an interplanetary rocket ship was, comparatively speaking, easy enough—though, as you can imagine, there were countless factors to be considered: weight, resistance to pressure and friction, how to produce oxygen for breathing, and so on. But all these things were easy of solution compared with the immense problem of finding a fuel—a fuel powerful enough to carry us right through the stratosphere and to give us enough impetus to take us to the gravity belt of the particular planet we proposed visiting: yet a fuel light enough and compact enough to allow of us storing sufficient of it in the rocket to be able to make a return flight to earth.

To cut a long story short, unexpected financial help came in the form of a legacy left to Dr. McGillivray by an uncle of his in America. We were overjoyed. The Doctor immediately gave up his job—he had been engaged in research work at Aberdeen University—and took a big house near Pitlochry, in Perthshire, as a workshop and experiment center. I, as it happened, had a smallish house near Pitlochry myself, where I used to retire when I had any writing to do. So I was able to see a great deal of the Doctor—indeed, I spent most of my time with him, tinkering in the laboratory, trying to understand the vast and endless formulæ he worked at in his study, talking and dreaming far into the night.

4

An Introduction

Eventually, a little more than a year ago, the Doctor announced to me that he had solved the fuel problem. I shall never forget his face as he confronted me over one of the immense retorts that crowded out the laboratory. It was evening, I remember—an evening in late autumn. The mists were over the high hills all round the house, but above the hills the sky was clear and bright. The Doctor's eyes were shining—it was almost as if there were tears in them—tears of sheer triumph. He stood there in his laboratory overalls, trembling a little from excitement, but very erect and dignified.

"I've done it, Steve," he said, in a low voice. "By heaven, man, I've done it! There's nothing to stop us now—we can go anywhere, anywhere!"

I thrilled to the depths. I listened to his breathless explanation, understanding only in part what he was telling me about the fuel. When he had finished I said:

"Mac—what are you going to do with it? How are you going to give it to the world—and when are you going to give it to the world?"

"Not yet, Steve," he said, after a pause, "not for a little while yet. We've got to be sure. Oh, I know the world! It's no use presenting it with theories, however perfect. It's got to be confronted with the *fait accompli*—it's got to see a thing done!"

"Mac—you mean——?"

"I mean, Steve, that you and I—only us two—are going on a journey! As soon as we can get things ready, we'll set off into space—to prove that this thing of mine works. I shall leave behind, when we go, a sealed envelope containing all our plans and formulæ, both for the ship and the fuel, with instructions that it is to be opened and the papers examined if we are not back by a certain date— that will show the world what we have attempted, at any rate. . . . Are you willing to come, Steve? I can't promise you anything, you know—this may be no more than a particularly spectacular way of committing suicide! . . ."

I looked at him for a long time in silence. My heart was beating strongly and I felt prickles—tremors—running over my spine. I moistened my lips.

"Mac—where are we going? The moon?"

He shook his head and raised his arm to point through the huge window of the laboratory to where, low down on the horizon, one star twinkled unsteadily, its color an unmistakable red, even to the naked eye.

"Mars!" I gasped.

"Yes, Mars! It is the one planet above all others that has excited and intrigued me since ever I first thought of this whole wild idea. It's the nearest of the planets, and it's the one, as you know, most likely to have life on it."

"You know what they call it," I said, "—the Angry Planet. . . . Mac, has it struck you that even if we do get there safely—if we reach it—we . . . we mightn't come back! We've no idea of what we may find. The creatures on it—if there are any—might be monsters— might tear us to pieces! . . ."

"I've thought of all that," he said quietly. "I've thought of almost everything. I go because I wish to prove that my rocket will work, and because I am curious, as a scientist, to know what sort of life there may be on other

6

planets besides the earth. I want you to come, Steve, because you're a writer—because you will be able to put down, in a way that I never could, something of what we may see. And I want you to come, too, because you are my friend, and have helped and encouraged me all along in my experiments. What do you say? Do we go to Mars?"

I looked at him steadily, then held out my hand.

"We go to Mars," I said.

We both turned and looked through the window again at the small, winking red eye of the Angry Planet, so many millions of miles away. . . .

Well, there it was. That is what we decided that autumn evening at Pitlochry. And thereafter began a period of intense activity. Endless arrangements had to be made, the rocket had to be built and equipped, every possible contingency had to be foreseen and accounted for.

Above all, we wanted the whole affair kept secret—publicity would be uncomfortable, and a hindrance. The Doctor had a few skilled laboratory assistants, and they helped us with the construction of the rocket itself—the *Albatross*, as the Doctor decided to call it; because, as he explained, it was a name full of the suggestion of voyages into strange and uncharted seas—it was associated with the Ancient Mariner, and we, heaven knows, were the most Modern of Mariners! The assistants worked to the Doctor's specifications, and had no idea that they were building anything as fantastic as a real space-ship—to them, it was just another rocket—such a rocket as they had made a hundred times for the Doctor, only bigger. They knew he was experimenting with rockets, and, if truth be told, regarded him, I believe, as not much more than an amiable crank. As long as their wages were paid —and they were, most royally—that was all they cared about.

We had reckoned that the work would take about a year to complete, but we toiled so hard, and were so inspired by our enthusiasm, that everything was ready, except for a few last touches, at the end of nine months —that is, at the beginning of this last summer. That was the position when, unexpectedly, at my cottage at Pitlochry, I got a letter from my married sister in London.

I will not take up space by quoting the letter in full— my sister was a garrulous woman—indeed, as the mother of Mike Malone, how could she have been otherwise? The main drift of it all was that her husband—some sort of big business man—was off suddenly on a special mission to South America—very important—and wanted her to go with him. Now, as it happened, her sister-in-law, who lived in Dorset somewhere, had fallen ill, and had asked my sister (her name was Marian, by the way) to look after her two children for a time at her house in London. So there were the children—all three of them— with nowhere to go. "And it struck me, darling Steve" (wrote Marian), "that it would be a grand and glorious idea to send them up to you in Pitlochry for a month or two. There you are, all alone in that house of yours, doing nothing else but writing (or whatever it is you do— I never have really known). It will be the very breath of life to you to have young people about the place. They're an absolutely delightful trio—Paul and Jacqueline (Margaret's children) are fourteen and twelve respectively, and my Mike—whom you haven't seen for two years, because you never deign to visit us, you old hermit—is eleven. They will be no trouble at all—Jacqueline, in fact, will be able to help your housekeeper with the chores—that is, if you've got a housekeeper at all: I wouldn't put it past you to do all your own catering, like the crank you are, and live on kippers and bread and cheese and endless bottles of beer. Do be a gem, Steve, and say you will have the children. I had planned to take them all down to Bournemouth or somewhere, but that is out of the question now that Arthur insists on my going out to South America with him—he says it's very important that I should, from the social point of view and all that sort of thing—you know how it is, dining with the wife of the firm's Chilean representative, etc., etc. (or is Chile not in South America?—I never know). The poor things—the children, not the Chilean representative and his wife—will be very very disappointed if they don't get a holiday, so do, do, do, Steve, say you will have them—I know they'd adore running about in the heather up there—it will make them very hardy and they'd simply *love* meeting the quaint people and hearing bagpipes and climbing mountains, etc. . . ." Thus Marian rambled on, for page after page. She finished with something quite fantastically typical: "I have booked sleepers for the children next Friday, so they should be with you on Saturday, i.e., a week to-day. I do hope it will be all right. I shall send you

9

some cards from the Argentine (if that's in South America as well as Chile). Your affectionate sister. Love and kisses. Marian. P.S.—Remember to see that Mike changes his socks if he gets wet in any of the bogs and things up there. P.P.S.—Never address him as Michael—he thinks it's girlish (I called him after Michael in Peter Pan, but he hates Peter Pan). He just likes plain Mike."

I simply did not know what to do about this letter. In one sense—because of the rocket, and the secrecy with which we had surrounded it—I did not want children running about the place. Yet there was no doubt I liked children, and I could not but agree with Marian that it would be a great pity for these three if they did not get a holiday after they had been promised one. After all, although the *Albatross* was finished and ready for the flight, the Doctor and I had not proposed setting off for some months. This meant that I was in a generally impatient mood, with nothing very concrete to do: I argued with myself that it would occupy my mind during the last weeks to have young companions about me. With care, the secret of the rocket could be kept from them, and they would be safely back in England and out of the way before the Doctor and I made the flight in the *Albatross*.

To crown all, Marian had said that the children were arriving on Saturday morning. It was Wednesday before her letter reached me at Pitlochry. There was hardly enough time to put the whole thing off without causing grievous disappointments. And so, in the end, on the Thursday, I wired to Marian:

"O.K. for children to stay. Will meet them Pitlochry

station Saturday morning. Love to the Chilean representative and wife. Steve."

The children came. They came not only to Perthshire, but, as the world knows, with me and the Doctor to Mars!

This introductory chapter has turned out to be longer than I had intended it to be. I would bring it to a quick end now, but there is one thing it strikes me I must explain, and that is why the Doctor and I set out on our adventure while the children were still in Scotland, thus making it possible for them to stow away with us on the *Albatross*.

One evening, about a week after the arrival of the children at Pitlochry, I went up to have a chat with the Doctor at his laboratory. I found him greatly agitated, pacing backwards and forwards among the apparatus with a scientific journal rolled up angrily in his hands.

"Why, Mac," I cried, "what's the matter? You look furious."

"I am furious," he barked, stopping in his pacing and confronting me. "Look at this, Steve—just look at it!"

He thrust the rolled-up journal into my hands. While I glanced through the article he indicated in bewilderment, not understanding in any detail the quaint farrage of symbols and algebraic signs it contained, he stormed on:

"Do you realize what it means, Steve? Kalkenbrenner's on the track—Kalkenbrenner of Chicago, you're bound to have heard of him. He's been doing some rocket experimenting for years—at one time I even had correspondence with him about an improved design in *tuyères* he was developing. And now, as you can see from that, he's busy along the same lines as I have been on the question of fuel—judging by that article he might even hit on my own principle at any moment. It's monstrous —monstrous!"

"My dear Mac," I remonstrated, "what will it matter if he does? It will only mean that you'll have confirmation that your idea is a good one."

"What will it matter?" he cried. "What will it matter? My dear Steve, where is your soul? Doesn't it mean anything to you that we should be first in the field? Haven't you any sense of the prestige of being one of the first men to leave the earth and go to another planet? If Kalkenbrenner does find my fuel principle his next step is obvious—he'll do what we have done and build a rocket—and set off to make a flight in it. . . . No, Steve, my boy, there's only one thing that all this means—it means that instead of waiting till our original date, you and I are setting off as soon as we can—to-morrow if it can be arranged—in any case, no later than the beginning of next week."

"Mac," I gasped, after a moment of dazed silence, "we couldn't—it's impossible! I mean—think of all those calculations of ours. You know as well as I do that we chose our original date because the orbits of earth and Mars brought the two planets to a suitable relationship for the flight at that time."

"I know that," he said. "But look here, Steve, I've been revising the calculations." He waved to an immense sheet of paper on the laboratory table which was covered with diagrams and equational calculations. "If we set out now, instead of three months hence, there's very little difference in the distance between us and Mars. As you know, Mars is 35 million miles away from us at her nearest, and something like 265 million miles away from us when her orbit takes her to the other side of the sun. She revolves in an orbit *outside* ours, don't forget. In a quarter of a year the arc of her orbit in relation to ours would place her the same distance from us, only on *the other side of us!* It's merely a matter of changing the direction of the rocket and adjusting one or two of the instruments—we can do that in a couple of hours. The only thing is——," and he looked at me solemnly, "we daren't wait too long —as I say, we must be off some time between now and the beginning of next week."

I was silent for a moment. Then I said:

"Mac, I'm with you. Whatever you say goes for me. This is your venture from the beginning—I feel myself only too privileged to be in on it with you at all. If you think, honestly, that we must start to-morrow, or the next day, then we start to-morrow or the next day. There's only one thing I must do—I must make some arrangements about disposing of these three children that are staying with me."

He threw up his hands in a gesture of despair.

"Children!" he cried. "Children! You'd delay the most remarkable journey ever made by man in the whole course of history for a covey of giggling children!"

"Now, Mac, have patience. Don't get over-excited and out of perspective. I'm not suggesting we should delay the journey—I'm only saying that I've got to think up something to do with the children, so that I can leave with you with a free conscience."

"Give them back to their mothers," he said gruffly. "That's where children ought to be—with their mothers."

"Their mother is ill," I said gently, "or rather, the mother of two of them is ill. The other one's mother is in South America, having dinner with the Chilean representative and his wife. . . . No. I'll have to send them somewhere else—not to their mothers."

"Don't you know anyone who is fond of children?" asked the Doctor impatiently.

"Well—there *is* that cousin of mine in Glasgow that I've often mentioned to you—Cross his name is. He and his wife have a couple of youngsters of their own, and they're always filling their house up with kittens and puppies and things. They must be reasonably attached to children. . . . I believe they'd take my lot in an emergency."

"Good," said the Doctor. "Then *that's* settled. Make your arrangements straight away, and I shall work out exactly when it will be best to launch the *Albatross*. I suspect it will be some time in the late afternoon either to-morrow or the day after—anyway, I'll let you know."

I walked home to my cottage, mentally composing a letter to my cousin as I went. It was full of such phrases as "Sorry to trouble you with such a burden at this extraordinarily short notice" . . . "Called away on most urgent and extremely important business" . . . and so on.

I wrote the letter the following morning. I had no

sooner finished it than there was a 'phone call from the Doctor.

"Steve," came his thin excited voice through the receiver, "it's this afternoon—this afternoon as ever is! We set off at 4.20. Can you make it?"

"I can make it," I said resignedly. "I'll be over about 3."

I looked at the letter to my cousin and sighed. It was now almost noon. The children had set off for a picnic among the hills about an hour before, taking luncheon sandwiches with them—they were not expected back till 6 o'clock at the earliest. As it happened, too, this was my housekeeper's day off (contrary to my sister's suspicions, I did have a housekeeper—a most amiable and sensible widow). She had gone to visit a sister at Crieff—I had no way of getting in touch with her.

In the end, I solved the problem by writing a note to my housekeeper and putting my letter to my cousin in the same envelope with it.

"Dear Mrs. Duthie," I said, "I have, I regret to say, been hastily summoned on urgent business. Will you, as soon as you can, send the children to my cousin, Mr. John Keir Cross, at 22, North Gardner Street, Glasgow, W.1, giving them the enclosed letter to deliver to him. Explain to the children that I have had to go off suddenly, and give them my love, and my apologies for having to interrupt their holiday and change their plans yet once again. You will find, in the top right-hand drawer of my writing-desk, enough money for the fares and for all your own immediate purposes. When this money is done, get in touch with my lawyer, whose address you know, **and** he will see that you are kept supplied."

I added a postscript which, I knew, would cause simple Mrs. Duthie endless speculation and worry:

"If I am not back at the cottage by six months from to-day, my lawyer will tell you what to do about giving up the house and so on."

I wrote one more note, to my lawyer himself. I had already lodged with him a sealed envelope containing all instructions concerning the disposition of my small capital and few possessions if I should not return. This present note was to tell him to open the sealed papers if he had not heard from me by the end of six months.

All this done, I made myself a light lunch. Then, at half-past two, I set off for the Doctor's laboratory. At the top of the hill I turned and looked back at my cottage. It was impossible not to feel a little sad and forlorn. I had been very happy in my small house, and perhaps this was the last I would ever see of it. Indeed, I thought, as I turned to look at Pitlochry itself, nestling among the hills to my right, this may be the last earthly landscape I shall ever gaze on: from now on—if I do see any land at all— it will be Martian land. And what that may be like, I do not know. . . .

My cousin never was burdened with the three children —he never read my carefully apologetic letter. Mrs. Duthie—poor soul!—came back from Crieff to find that not only had I been called away on urgent business, **but,** apparently, so had the children.

An Introduction

What happened was simplicity itself—and yet, as you will see, it was as wild and complicated in the end as any dream ever was.

I said, earlier, that the children have helped to write this book. The way it has turned out is this: After our return to earth, and when the turmoil and excitement had died down, we all—that is, myself, the Doctor, Paul, Jacqueline, and Mike—returned to my cottage for a rest. I suggested that during this rest, and while things were still fresh in our minds, we might well occupy ourselves by writing down some account of our remarkable adventures—the idea was that we were each to write various chapters of a book, setting forth the aspects of the adventure that particularly concerned us. Even the Doctor agreed to contribute (in non-technical language) an occasional paper.

We did so. It is this book you are now reading. Apart from altering an occasional spelling and punctuation fault (particularly in Mike's somewhat flowery manuscripts!), I have left the children's chapters mostly as they wrote them. All I have done is to arrange our various contributions and fragments so as to present a reasonably coherent story.

With these words of explanation, then, I close this, my own first contribution to our book. I pass the cloak of the narrator to Mr. Paul Adam, who now presents to you Chapter II.

CHAPTER II. A HOLIDAY IN SCOT-
LAND, BY PAUL ADAM

MY NAME is Paul Adam and I am the oldest of
the three of us who went to Mars with Dr. McGillivray
and Mr. Stephen MacFarlane. The other two were my
young sister Jacqueline (we always call her Jacky) and our
cousin Mike Malone.

Our Uncle Steve—that is what we call Mr. MacFarlane,
though he is only Mike's uncle really and not mine's and
Jacky's—suggested I should write down how we got on to
the *Albatross*. Doctor Mac's space-ship. So here goes.
(Mike and Jacky are looking over my shoulder, so they
will keep me right and see I don't make any mistakes in
the story.)

I'd better begin at the point when we got to Uncle
Steve's house at Pitlochry for our holiday last summer.

A Holiday in Scotland

We were all very excited. Everything had been arranged so quickly, and it was wonderful to set out on such a long journey—over 500 miles—all by ourselves. We had once met Uncle Steve at our Aunt Marian's house in London and from what we remembered of him it looked as if we would have a great holiday. For one thing, he was good at telling stories, we remembered (he is a writer, so his head is full of stories), and we reckoned that even if it rained all the time, the way people say it does in Scotland, then it wouldn't much matter, for we could sit round the fire and listen to stories.

Well, after a good journey we reached Pitlochry and Uncle Steve met us at the station. Then we drove to his cottage in a little pony trap (Mike was allowed to hold the reins for part of the way) and we had a whopping great breakfast which Mrs. Duthie, the housekeeper, had got ready for us. There was porridge with cream—we had never tasted real Scots porridge before, and it was won-derful—then herrings dipped in oatmeal and fried, and then hot oatcakes with masses of fresh butter and real heather honey.

That first day we didn't do very much but just lounge about Uncle Steve's garden, though in the evening we did do a little exploring in the woods, and Uncle Steve introduced us to an old gamekeeper with a beard and lots of bright colored fish-hooks stuck all over his hat (which had a peak at the front and back, just like the hat that Sherlock Holmes used to wear, and flaps that went over your ears when it was cold, though when it wasn't cold you folded them up and they were buttoned on the top).

19

This old man, whose name was McIntosh, promised he would take us out fishing and rabbit shooting and all sorts of things like that. He had a real beauty of a double-barreled gun under his armpit—or rather his oxter, as he and Mrs. Duthie called it—and two wonderful dogs named Lass and Luath.

The next day was a Sunday, and in the morning we went into Pitlochry to Church in the little pony trap. In the afternoon we all went for a walk, and Uncle Steve took us to a big house which he said belonged to a great friend of his. This was Dr. McGillivray. We liked him very much indeed from the first go-off. On our way to see him Uncle Steve had told us that he was not a Doctor because he went around attending to sick people, or anything like that, but because he had studied Philosophy. So we thought, you see, that he would be old and have a long beard, and would be absent-minded and all that sort of thing. But he wasn't—he was really quite young, and was great fun. There were all sorts of gadgets in his house, and Mike and I had a wonderful time. There was an old Wimhurst machine and we made sparks jump on to our fingers—oh, a good two or three inches long, they were— and a little electric shocking coil that we persuaded Jacky to try, and then we switched on the current suddenly and sent her jumping right across the room (it was perfectly harmless, of course—in fact, Doctor Mac said that a mild shock like that was very good for you).

After tea in the Doctor's study (which was full of hundreds and hundreds of books), Uncle Steve said that he and Doctor Mac had something very important to dis-

McIntosh, the gamekeeper

cuss. So they went through to a different part of the house which they called the laboratory, and we were given permission to go out into the grounds for a stroll.

Well, it was now we got our first impression that our holiday was going to be exciting, and that there was something mysterious and well worth finding out about going on between Doctor Mac and Uncle Steve.

At the back of the Doctor's house, just beyond the part they called the laboratory, there was a little wood, or copse, of fir trees. We were strolling here "quite joco," as Mrs. Duthie would say, when suddenly the trees stopped, and there in front of us was an enormous high wooden enclosure—a sort of palisade, like the one in *Treasure Island*, only much much bigger. It was as high as a good-sized house, and at least two hundred feet square (Mike paced it out, and each side was 110 paces, and we always used to reckon one of Mike's measuring steps as a little over two feet).

"Hullo, what's this?" said Mike.

"It's some sort of house," said Jacky.

"House my foot," I chimed in. "Whoever built a house that size? Besides, it hasn't any roof—and where are the windows?"

"Well, they might be going to add a roof—you never know," said Jacky sulkily. "And maybe it's a special new type of house without windows. They're up to all sort of experiments these days."

While we were arguing like this, young Mike was searching all over the palisade for some gap or knot-hole to peer through. He now gave a cry to indicate he had found one.

"I say, just come and have a look at this," he yelled. "What on earth do you suppose it can be?"

We went over beside him and I bent down and looked through the hole. Unfortunately, it was a very little hole, but I was able to see enough through it to thoroughly whet my curiosity. (Jacky has just stopped me to say I've used a split infinitive and that that is bad grammar. I should have written "thoroughly to whet my curiosity," or "to whet my curiosity thoroughly." Well, it doesn't much matter—you'll know what I mean, and that's the main thing.)

Now, where was I?—oh yes, the thing inside the enclosure. It was, as far as I could see, an immense sort of shell, like the fuselage of a huge aeroplane, and it was made of some sort of metal, very highly polished, so that it shone in the sunshine. Every now and again, in the wall of it, there were small round windows, like port-holes in a ship, only they seemed of enormously thick glass, and bulged a great deal, like Mrs. Duthie's spectacles. It was lying, as far as I could judge, on a big wooden platform that was inclined at an angle of about forty degrees. I could not see far enough to my left or right through the knot-hole to be able to get any sort of glimpse of the ends of the thing.

"It looks like a boat, almost," I said, looking round at Mike, while Jacky had a turn at the knot-hole.

"That's exactly what I thought," nodded Mike. "And it's on a sort of big slipway, like a kind of launching ramp. But where's the water? There isn't any water for miles."

"If only we could see properly," grumbled Jacky. "This knot-hole is no good. Can't you find a bigger one, Mike?"

Mike stood looking thoughtful for a moment. He has a way of standing with his arms akimbo, seeking what he calls "inspiration." Then, when it arrives, he hits his brow a great smack. This is what he did now.

"I've got it," he cried. "Paul, I'm going up one of these trees. Then I'll be able to see in over the top of the wall. Give me a hoist up, will you?"

We chose one of the highest of the trees, and Mike was up it in an instant, like the young ape we have always said he was. We could see him from below clinging on to one of the slender top branches of the fir, and craning his neck to peer into the enclosure. He gave a long low whistle of excitement.

I was just getting ready to swarm up one of the other trees myself, when Jacky, who was standing a little distance away, came running over to me to say that she could see through the trees that Doctor Mac and Uncle Steve had come out of the laboratory and were strolling back towards the study across the lawn, very deep in conversation.

"And it just struck me," she added, "that this thing, whatever it is, must be pretty secret, or they wouldn't have shoved the wall round it. I think we'd better not be found looking in at it—I vote we go and join the two of them, and we can come back some other time and explore this whole place properly."

I agreed that this was a good idea and we whistled to Mike to come down. Uncle Steve and the Doctor had gone into the study through the French windows by the time we emerged from the wood. On our way across the lawn, Mike explained to us in an excited low voice what he had seen from the tree-top.

"It's immense," he said. "You never saw anything like it—honest you didn't. It goes very tapery and pointed to one end—the end low down on the ramp—and it bulges up to a big round sort of head at the other end—it's exactly like an enormous pear. And there are all sorts of little nozzles, like guns, sticking out all over it—a great mass of them at the pointed end, one or two along the sides, and then some more at the blunt end, though not so many as at the pointed end. There's a ladder goes up to a big doorway in the side near the bulgy end—if you two hadn't called me down I'd have thought out some way of getting over the wall to find out what it's like inside."

By this time we had reached the study. Uncle Steve and Doctor Mac were talking very earnestly and quietly together. They broke off when we went in through the French windows, and after a few moments of chatting, Uncle Steve said that it was time we were thinking of getting back home. So we said cheerio to Doctor Mac and set off.

As we walked through the fields to the cottage, I said to Uncle Steve in an innocent voice:

"By the way, Uncle Steve, we were walking about in

the woods up at Doctor Mac's house, and we came across a big sort of wooden enclosure thing. What's it for?"

Uncle Steve looked a bit uncomfortable.

"Oh, that," he said. "Yes. . . . Well, you see, that's really a secret, you know. The Doctor is carrying out some very special scientific experiments that nobody's supposed to know anything about, and that's one of the places where he works at them."

"What sort of experiments?" asked Mike. "They must be very odd if he needs a great big place like that for them."

"Oh, just experiments, you know," said Uncle Steve, getting more and more embarrassed. "As a matter of fact, you're not really supposed to have gone into the wood at all—I should have told you it's out of bounds. Next time you see the Doctor you had better not mention you were there—he's very touchy about his work."

And he suddenly changed the subject to talk about our holiday plans for the next day. So we knew we were on to something. We all three of us looked at each other and gave a secret smile, and Mike winked.

For the next few days nothing much happened. We had a good enough time among the hills and so on, but there was nothing spectacular. I thought a lot about what we had seen in the enclosure, and wondered often what Doctor Mac's experiments could be. And I knew that Mike was doing the same.

One thing that added to the mystery of it all was the behavior of Uncle Steve. He seemed to have something on his mind. He went very often to see Doctor Mac, then when he came home he would sit for hours just thinking —sitting in the evenings at the window simply staring at the sky. One night it rained very badly and we had to stay indoors. We half-expected he would read or tell us some of his stories, or at least do something to entertain us. But no—he sat in a corner all the time, brooding and chewing at his pipe-stem, and Mike and I were forced to play draughts, while Jacky got on with a bit of sewing.

Then suddenly, one evening, while Jacky and I were sitting reading in a little summer-house sort of place right at the foot of Uncle Steve's garden, Mike came rushing up to us with his face all red with excitement.

"I've got it!" he yelled, slapping his brow like a little lunatic. "Oh boy, I know what that thing up at the Doc's place is! It's a rocket!"

"A rocket?" I said. Mike nodded, and Jacky stared at him as if he'd gone off his nut.

(*Insert note by Jacqueline Adam:* I'm putting a note in here because Paul keeps on thinking he can do his big brother stuff and make me out as if I were stupid. Well, I'm not. I didn't say anything when Mike told us about Doctor Mac's rocket, because I had suspected it was a rocket all along, so there—and that's more than Paul ever did!—J.A.)

"Yes, a rocket," went on Mike. "The old Doctor's been experimenting with them a long time. It was Mr. McIntosh, the gamekeeper, that told me," he continued. "Some of the Doctor's laboratory assistants are in lodgings with his sister in Pitlochry, and they let him into the secret. They've been building experimental rockets for the Doctor for years—though this is the biggest one ever. They think he's a little bit dotty, as a matter of fact."

By this time I had realized the full weight of what it was that Mike was telling us.

"Phew!" I gasped, "a rocket! Well, my hat, if he's building a rocket as big as that, he must be hoping to reach the moon at the very least! I say, Mike—what an idea! Do you suppose maybe he *is* thinking of trying to reach the moon?"

"He couldn't," said Jacky. "Don't be silly!"

"You never know," muttered Mike (who was on my side the moment he saw that Jacky wasn't—that's always the way with us three). "Scientists are experimenting in some mighty queer things these days."

He stood for a moment with his arms akimbo, then suddenly he slapped his brow again.

"Anyway," he cried, "I'm going to have a closer look at that thing. And I'll tell you when—to-morrow!"

"To-morrow?"

"Yes—to-morrow."

"But we're going for a picnic to-morrow," said Jacky. "Don't you remember? It's Mrs. Duthie's day off, but she's making us some sandwiches before she goes to Crieff to see her sister, and we're going into the hills at about 11 o'clock."

"I know," nodded Mike. "And I for one am coming back from the hills early in the afternoon. *And* I'm going round by the Doctor's house. *And* I'm going to sneak in through the back way to the little wood. *And* I'm going to have a long rope with me, with a big hook at one end—a sort of grappling iron, see. And if it's the last thing I do I'm going over that wall to have a look at that rocket."

"Don't be silly, Mike," said Jacky. "You'll get into trouble. Uncle Steve told us that Doctor Mac is very touchy about his work. Besides, the laboratory men will be there tomorrow afternoon."

"Not them," said Mike triumphantly. "That's another thing Mr. McIntosh told me. The laboratory men were paid off to-day—they've finished working for the Doctor altogether."

"Well then, the Doctor will be there himself—probably with Uncle Steve, too."

"Not if we go about 4 o'clock. That's why I'm suggesting the afternoon instead of the morning—it's the one time we are likely to be undisturbed. Don't you remember what the Doc said last Sunday?—that he wouldn't miss his tea at 4 o'clock for anything. He and Uncle Steve will be in the house at that time. . . . Anyway, I'm jolly well going to have a shot at it—and if you two aren't with me, well that's just too bad—I'll have to go by myself, that's all."

He shut up then, as close as an oyster. And Jacky and I just knew from experience that as far as Mike was concerned there was simply nothing more to be said.

To cut a long story short, as they say in books (but after all, I've turned into a writer myself, so why shouldn't I say it too?), the next afternoon, at about 3:45, the three of us crawled through the wood at the Doctor's house, very stealthily and silently. We had been up in the hills since 11 o'clock, but all through the picnic there had been a kind of suspense in us, and an impatience to get on with our plan. That plan was to sneak in over the wall, have a close look at the rocket to satisfy our curiosity, then get out again, hang about for a bit, and finally turn up at Uncle Steve's cottage at about 6 o'clock—the time we had said we'd be back from the picnic—as if nothing had happened.

When we got to the wall, Mike went up to the little knot-hole we knew of. First of all he peered through it, then he listened at it.

"I was right," he said in a gleeful whisper. "Not a soul about. I'm going up."

He unwrapped a long thin rope from about his waist. Then he took an ugly big hook out of his haversack (it was an outsize salmon gaff that he had borrowed from old Mr. McIntosh) and tied it to one end of the rope with—as he explained—a real unslippable sailor's knot.

He slung the hook up into the air, and after a couple of tries it caught firmly on the wood at the top of the enclosure wall. Then, after spitting on his hands, Mike clambered up, using his feet on the wall and pulling on the rope—the way natives go up coconut palms, as I expect you've seen in the movies.

When he got up, he sat straddle-wise on top and whispered down:

"All clear. Come on, Paul—you next. And hurry up about it."

I went up. Then Jacky followed, Mike and I hauling

on the rope to give her a hand. Then we lowered Jacky down the other side, and then I went down, and finally Mike. There we were, in the enclosure, with Doctor Mac's rocket in front of us!

"I say," said Mike, in an awed whisper. "What a monster!"

"It's beautiful," sighed Jacky, "it's simply beautiful!"

It certainly was. It was huge, like a great shining silver fish, all sparkling in the sun. As Mike had said, it was pear-shaped. All down the back of it there was a long slender fin. Judging from what we knew to be the length of the enclosure, it was a good 150 feet long.

We stared and stared. Then Mike said, in a puzzled voice:

"I say—it's facing a different way from what it was last Sunday—and it's much more tilted up into the air. That ramp it's on must be adjustable—probably there's a little donkey engine or something to work it. That means the door is on the other side now—come on, I'm going round."

We went round by the bulging end, which soared high into the air above us—almost perpendicularly, it seemed. As we got to the front we saw two enormous windows (like the ones all along the sides I have already mentioned, only much bigger). They seemed like huge shining eyes. Painted in a semi-circle between them, in silver, were the words: THE ALBATROSS.

"Lovely," said Jacky softly. "What a perfect name for it! It's the loveliest thing I've ever seen. I don't know whether it's meant to go to the moon or not, but it certainly *deserves* to go to the moon!"

When we got round to the other side we saw that in that part of the enclosure there were a great many sheds and lean-to shelters against the wall. Inside them we could see some machinery—lathes and so on—so we took these to be the workshops. Also on this side of the enclosure there was an immense gate in the wall, but this, of course, was closed.

High up in the rocket on this side, near the huge blunt nose, there was a big metal door, wide open. Suspended from it was a slender ladder of flexible steel. Before we could say a word, Mike was half-way up it.

"Mike!" called Jacky. "There'll be trouble! You can't do it!"

"Oh, can't I!" he yelled back, and gave one of his guffaws of triumph. "Come on, the two of you, while you have the chance. Don't be a couple of sissies!"

By this time he had reached the top and had disappeared inside the rocket. I looked at Jacky and she looked at me.

"Oh well!" she said. "We might as well be hanged for sheep as lambs."

And she started to climb, too. And when she was almost at the top, I followed her.

We found ourselves, when we got through the outer door, confronted, over a gap of about two feet, by another door, which was also open, though this one opened inwards. I saw, immediately, looking along to my left and right from the little bridge or gangway, why this was: the outside of the rocket was a huge casing-shell—a sort of skin, or envelope: the whole thing was like a gigantic thermos flask, with an inner chamber—the two parts separated, as I saw, with massive springs.

Inside the inner door we were in a huge cabin. It must have been pivoted in some way to the inner shell, for in spite of the angle at which the rocket lay, the floor of it was level, and parallel to the ground.

I can't begin to describe what this cabin was like at a first glance. There was, at one end of it, a huge panel of controls—wheels, levers, dials covered with figures, switches, resistance coils, valves, and so on. Two small windows were let into this panel, and through them we could see across the space between the inner and outer shells and so through the two huge eyes in the front of the *Albatross*. There were small windows in the side walls of the cabin, too, that gave on the portholes down the side of the rocket. In the back wall of the cabin were several steel doors—we opened one of them and found a small cupboard full of cardboard boxes. These boxes, when we had a look inside them, proved to our surprise to contain thousands and thousands of tubes of tooth-paste! Mike and I were puzzling what on earth anyone could want so much tooth-paste on a rocket for, when suddenly there came an excited yelp from Jacky, who was over by the cabin door.

"Mike—Paul," she said, "we're trapped! They're coming—Uncle Steve and the Doctor are coming in!"

We rushed over beside her. Far below, the big gate in the palisade had been swung open, and Uncle Steve and

Doctor Mac were walking from it across to the ladder of the rocket!

"Good Lord!" I gasped. "Now there's going to be trouble! What on earth can we say?"

"We needn't say anything," said Mike in a whisper. "Ten to one they're only coming for a look over. They can't stay all night—Uncle Steve is expecting us at the cottage at 6, don't forget. I vote we get into that toothpaste cupboard and hide—it's big enough for the three of us—and with luck we'll get away with it. Come on!"

We rushed across the cabin and crowded into the cupboard. We got the door shut in the nick of time—as I pulled it to behind us, I heard Uncle Steve and the Doctor at the top of the ladder.

We huddled together, hardly daring to breathe. It was pitch dark. Through the steel door we could hear, in a muffled way, the movements of Uncle Steve and the Doctor. First there were two loud clanging noises, then a sound of hissing, quite strong at first, but getting fainter. I pressed my ear to the door and could just hear the Doctor and Uncle Steve speaking.

There were only two short speeches. After a long pause, Doctor Mac said (and even through the steel door I could hear an awful sort of excitement in his voice):

"Well, Steve, this is it—this is it at last!"

And Uncle Steve said:

"Yes, this is it, Mac." Then he added, in a queer, half-choking voice: "Good-bye, old earth—good-bye! . . ."

Then there was another pause. Then a slight whirring noise. And then—

34

A Holiday in Scotland

An immense, explosive, rushing sound! And I felt, suddenly, as if my ears would burst. And there was a terrible, terrible pressure on my chest—it was as if, suddenly, I weighed hundreds and thousands of pounds!

And then everything went black. I—all three of us, as I learned later—lost consciousness. . . .

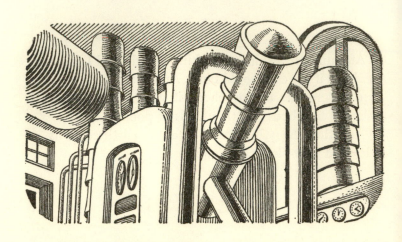

CHAPTER III. SOME PARENTHETICAL REMARKS BY ANDREW McGILLIVRAY, Ph.D., F.R.S., ON ROCKETS AND SPACE-SHIPS IN GENERAL, AND THE ALBATROSS IN PARTICULAR

MY FRIEND, Mr. Stephen MacFarlane, has asked me to contribute an occasional paper to this volume, an obligation which I hasten to fulfill with the greatest of pleasure. He has also asked me to keep my remarks short, and to couch them in a language that will be quite comprehensible to the most completely lay mind. This part of the commitment I view with some dismay. I am, after all, a scientist, and a scientist who has

36

specialized in a particularly complex subject. It is almost impossible, I feel compelled to say, for me to write comfortably about this subject in what I might call an *elementary* way. In one sense, anything of value I might say would *necessarily* be completely unintelligible to the lay mind that Mr. MacFarlane talks of! However, on the understanding that these remarks are to be regarded as doing no more than skim the surface of a vast subject, I hasten to perform what my friend has asked of me. Any who wish to pursue the topic further—to delve into the finer technicalities—are referred to the numerous contributions I have made to the better-known scientific journals since the return of the *Albatross* to earth.

With this preamble, then, let me begin by saying that I was first attracted to serious experimentation with rockets some fourteen or fifteen years ago. Before that, I knew what the normally well-educated man might be expected to know on the subject—that rockets were more than mere Guy Fawkes toys: that the principle behind them was possible of application to the aeroplane—the flying machine: that there were even in the world some wild and daring souls who dreamed of traveling, by means of rockets, not only into and through the stratosphere, but to the moon—and even beyond the moon. One day, however, I met, on a train journey, a young man who told me that he had just come back from a tour of Germany, where he had seen some truly remarkable experiments with small mail-carrying rockets, and even one that had transported, it was alleged, an intrepid human traveler some six miles into the stratosphere. I was so impressed by what he told me that I read all the available literature on the subject, and in a very short space of time I became so enthralled by it that I could barely think of anything else. The more I studied, the more convinced I became that rocket flights of greater and greater distances would be possible in the future. I grew to believe that journeys through space to the moon and the planets were not such illusory dreams after all—in short, I joined the band of "wild and daring souls" I have just referred to.

Mr. MacFarlane has told, elsewhere in this book, how he helped me in my experiments with his savings—how, eventually, my coming into a considerable legacy made it possible for me to devote myself completely to the whole immense subject.

I will not weary you with an account in detail of my innumerable attempts and failures at building a ship to go through space—such a catalogue would be of interest only to the specialist. It will suffice to say that as I went on I grew more and more enthusiastic. One by one I solved the various problems—each experiment taught me something new. I learned, gradually, what shape my rocket would have to be, how I could overcome such problems as insulation (from the tremendous friction of the atmosphere in the initial part of the flight), how I could slow down my space-ship at the end of a journey and effect an easy and comfortable landing, and so on and so on. Through it all, behind and beyond every experiment, lay the real problem, the immense, the overwhelming difficulty: fuel.

Some Parenthetical Remarks

Let me embark here on a short explanation of what is entailed in a space flight.

In order to cover the immense distances involved—Mars, for instance, is 35,000,000 miles away at its nearest to earth, and the moon, the closest of all the heavenly bodies, is some 239,000 miles distant—in order, as I say, to cover these vast spaces, a truly colossal initial speed is required of the rocket. Yet, by a paradox, the *propelling power is not required to function throughout the entire journey.* If sufficient speed can be engendered on leaving the earth, the motors can be switched off once the machine is free of the earth's atmosphere, and thereafter the rocket will continue traveling—through infinity, in fact, if nothing is done to control it.

The trouble is, however, that the human body cannot stand too great a sudden speed. If the rocket left the earth at the final speed necessary, the travelers in it would be struck dead immediately. What, then, can be done?

Fortunately, the pull of the earth's gravity lessens as one gets more and more distant from the center of it. Suppose that the pull of gravity on the earth's surface (which is about 4,000 miles from the center) is represented by the unit 1. Then, at 4,000 miles from the surface—i.e., twice this distance from the center—the pull would be 1/4th. At 8,000 miles—three times the distance—it would be 1/9th—in short (if I may be permitted by Mr. MacFarlane to say so!) the force of gravity varies as the square of the distance.

All this, in brief, means that it is possible to visualize starting off from the actual surface of the earth at a speed

39

that can, without too much discomfort, be borne by the human body. Then at some distance from the surface, when everything—including the human body—is very much lighter, and consequently not subject to the fatal increase of pressure, the speed can be stepped up. By the time the earth's atmosphere is left behind—about 200 miles at least from the surface—the total desired speed may be begun to be reached without discomfort—a speed well above the pull of gravity (seven miles per second). It is now that the motors can be shut off, and the machine will go on traveling.

This delayed acceleration has the additional advantage that the rocket is not traveling at so great a speed through the 200 miles atmosphere belt as to be burned up by friction.

The principle that I have just outlined is the real secret of the success of the *Albatross*. It is so designed that there are *two fuels in operation:* one to give the initial start-off, and a second to provide the tremendous acceleration required before launching into space itself.

It is this second fuel that is my own patent—it is this that I regard as the keynote of my whole invention. The first fuel is, I can say frankly, a highly concentrated essence of acetylene gas. The second fuel I cannot in any detail describe, without becoming outrageously technical. Briefly, it is an adaptation of atomic hydrogen—a method of making that most dangerous of substances quite manageable.

It is capable of developing enormous power in a very short space of time. And above all, it is light and easily packed, so that enough can be stored and carried in the rocket for the return journey.

So much for the main problems of space flight, overcome, as we have been able to demonstrate, in the *Albatross*. Minor difficulties—such as that of providing a supply of breathable air for the journey (a problem already solved in general by submarine designers)—were dealt with as the ship was built. I will not here say anything about the innumerable calculations it was necessary for me to make to be able to assure myself that once the *Albatross* was traveling in space it would go in such a direction as to fall into the gravitational pull of Mars. These are abstruse things, not capable of being dealt with in a paper that has to conform to the limitations Mr. MacFarlane has set on it!

There is only one picturesque detail I would like to mention before closing this first brief essay, and that is that one problem that worried me quite considerably for a time was: what if, during the 35,000,000 mile journey, we collided with a meteor? These are, as is well known, very small—most of them are no bigger than golf balls, while some are mere grains of dust. At the same time, although they are so tiny, there is no doubt that because of their incredible velocity, they would go right through a space-ship if there were a collision: and the kinetic energy released by the impact would, more than probably, destroy the ship on the instant. For a time, as I say, I was worried by this vision—what was the use, I argued, of expending endless ingenuity in devising a rocket if it were going to be exploded by a pebble? However, in the end,

I realized that the whole thing was worth risking. Space is so vast that in spite of the billions of meteors in it, the chances of a direct hit on a space-ship (and I was able to prove it irrefutably by mathematical calculation) are only *one in a million!*

I feel that these few remarks conform to Mr. MacFarlane's requirements: namely, that I should write intelligibly for lay readers, stating the general problems of space flight and how they were solved in the *Albatross*: and, secondly, that I should be brief. I now—feeling that this is barely more than an interlude (and one that, to my own mind, might well have been dispensed with)—I now pass the pen to those more qualified than I to continue with the actual narrative part of this book.

CHAPTER IV. IMPRESSIONS OF A JOURNEY THROUGH SPACE, BY VARIOUS HANDS

I PREFACE this collection of short contributions and fragments on what it felt like to travel through space, with a brief account of how we found the children in what they called the "tooth-paste cupboard." (It is, as you will have gathered, Stepen MacFarlane writing again.)

The Doctor and I, expecting the sudden impression of weight that would assail us on the start-off of the *Albatross*, lay down on two highly-sprung mattresses we had prepared for the purpose just before the Doctor touched the lever to launch the space-ship. We also wore masks, specially designed by the Doctor, that pumped oxygen into our lungs automatically. In these ways we hoped to

43

overcome to an extent the uncomfortable effects of the shock of leaving earth.

Nevertheless, my first feeling after seeing the Doctor press the lever, was that someone had bound steel chains round my chest and was constricting them, as it were, with a monstrous tourniquet. My head swam—there were alternating flashes of colored light and darkness before my eyes. I felt as if I weighed hundreds of pounds. I had hoped to be able to keep my gaze fixed through one of the lower side windows of the *Albatross*, so that I could see the earth receding from us. But I found this to be quite impossible. When my sight did clear, and my head ceased pounding, all I could see below us was a white swirling mist—a sort of milkiness—with, occasionally shining through it, pale patches of indistinct green and blue.

The first feeling of heavy helplessness seemed to last for at least half an hour; but, as it passed, I looked at the special clock that was set into the instrument panel and saw that it had lasted barely one and a half minutes. (Incidentally, I may say here in passing that because of the complete weightlessness that affected everything in the rocket once we got into outer space, this clock—although it had been specially designed by the Doctor, as I say—absolutely refused to function: we had no real idea throughout the journey what time it was—though, as you will see, we did manage to get a notion whether it was day or night.)

We were well through the stratosphere and it was time for the second fuel—the Doctor's patent—to be set off.

A Journey Through Space

I saw the Doctor rise from his mattress and, clinging to one of the special hand-rails, creep along the instrument panel. He took off his mask (we had started the oxygen apparatus before leaving, and the cabin was full of good breathable air) and signaled me to do the same. I did so.

"I'm setting off the second fuel," said the Doctor, his voice sounding thin and distant in my ears, which were still buzzing a little. "Better get into the foot-straps—or better still, put on the magnetic boots."

I nodded. The moment the second fuel was touched off we would achieve a speed wildly beyond the speed of gravity. Everything in the rocket would lose weight, ourselves included. To counteract this, the Doctor had provided straps at strategic points on the floor of the cabin into which we could slip our feet. He had also made several pairs of powerfully magnetized boots so that we could walk about. The principle was very simple. As you tugged at one foot in a walking movement, the slight jerk cut the magnetizing current and so you could lift that foot and take a step. Then, when you put the foot down again, contact was made in the sole inside by the muscular pressure, and the magnet gripped the steel floor again. I now, as the Doctor adjusted his controls, hastily put on a pair of these boots.

"Are you ready, Steve?" called the Doctor.

"All ready, Mac," I replied.

He touched a switch. Immediately there was a powerful shuddering all through the ship. And simultaneously there was, all through me, an indescribably strange throbbing, and another attack of dizziness—but a totally different kind of dizziness this time: an incredible sense of utter lightness. I made to shout something to the Doctor, but my tongue seemed to be waving freely in my mouth like a little fluttering flag and my lips were loose and flaccid and quite uncontrollable. In a few seconds this attack lessened and I was able to say something, although it was with the utmost difficulty at first that I was able to articulate.

"Mac," I cried, "this is incredible! This odd sort of throbbing—I've never experienced a sensation like this before."

"It'll pass in a moment," he called back. "You'll soon adjust yourself. It's the heart—it's been used to pumping blood all over you—a considerable weight in blood: and now all of a sudden your blood doesn't weigh anything at all. Your poor old heart is just a little bit bewildered, that's all!"

He chuckled. He was in the highest spirits—it was obvious that the *Albatross's* performance was exceeding all his expectations. He stood with his feet firmly dug into a pair of the floor-straps, examining the scores of dials on the control panel.

"I'd hate to tell you the speed we're traveling at, Steve," he cried. "Faster than any human beings have ever traveled before! In a few hours we'll be able to see the earth as a globe, man! Think of it—*as a globe!*"

I grinned at him. I caught the infection of his enthusiasm. I raised my hand to wave at him cheerily, and then suddenly had to burst out laughing. I had meant to raise it to my forehead in a sort of mock salute—instead, without my being able to control it at all, it shot right up above my head as far as it would go—and hung there, like something that was no part of me at all, wavering slightly in the air. I hauled it down. For a moment or two I stood there, practicing muscular control. I found that in a very short time I could adjust my muscular exertions, so that I could move my completely weightless fingers, arms, hands, and so on, in a reasonably normal way. By now my head had cleared, and the throbbing of my heart had stopped—I felt fine: elated, a little light-headed, as if I had just had a glass of champagne.

"Another few seconds and I shut off the motors," said the Doctor. "We have almost all the speed we need now, and we're well clear of the atmosphere. I say, Steve, could you go over and fetch me a pair of those boots from the locker?"

I was just moving across the cabin when, all of a sudden, and to our intense surprise, we heard the sound of hammering coming from behind the door of one of our small store closets at the back of the cabin. And, incredibly, there came to our ears very thin and muffled voices.

"Uncle Steve," they called, "Uncle Steve! Let us out, let us out!"

I stared at Mac and he stared at me. Even as I moved clumsily across the cabin to the door in my magnetic boots, a horrible suspicion was forming in my mind.

I had almost reached the door when it suddenly wafted open (it was weightless, like everything else, and its movement can best be described as like the movement in a slow motion film). And I had the strangest surprise of my life.

Out of the open doorway floated—literally floated!—the three children I had made such elaborate plans to dispose of to my cousin in Glasgow! They were white and shaken—that much I could see as they drifted past me. Their eyes had a dazed look. They moved their arms and legs in a stupid, drunken sort of way. And all the time they floated and bounced about the cabin like little balloons. For a moment one of them would rest on the floor or against one of the walls—then, at a slight involuntary muscular movement, they would shoot off at an angle and bump gently on the ceiling. They were yelling and calling me to catch them and hold them. It was a grotesque, an idiotic sight!

"Good Lord!" I yelled. "Mike—Jacky—Paul!—what in the name of all that's wonderful are you doing here?"

"We didn't mean it," shouted Mike from the ceiling. "We only came in to explore. We'd no idea you were going to—ouch!"

This exclamation came as he suddenly floated away from the ceiling and collided with Paul, who was moving in a gentle glide diagonally across the cabin. Jacky simultaneously drifted past me and I made a grab at her. But the movement she made to grab at me in return sent her shooting off at an angle, and next thing I saw she was right up in one of the corners of the cabin looking as if she was about to burst into tears.

By this time Mac had recovered from his amazement at seeing the children.

48

"Steve!" he cried, "for heaven's sake get hold of them
—do something! They'll smash up my instruments!"

He made a wild lunge at Paul, who was hovering just
over his head, and as he did so his feet came away from
the floor-straps. And he—Andrew McGillivray, Ph.D.,
F.R.S., of Aberdeen, Scotland—went soaring up to join
the human balloons in the air of the cabin! I alone of the
party remained on my feet. And, surveying the fantastic
scene, I burst into laughter. It was, undoubtedly, the
funniest thing I have ever seen.

The Doctor was the first to get back to normal. He
suddenly cried: "The motor, Steve—shut it off! It's past
time—if we don't stop it we'll develop too much speed,
and we'll use more of the fuel than we ought to, and
won't have enough for the return flight."

This sobered me. I started to plod across to the control panel. Before I got there, however, Mac managed to
push himself down from the ceiling to one of the hand-
rails, and groped his way by means of that to the motor
switch and put it off. The children, too, by this time, were
beginning to get some slight control into their movements. Paul had come to earth, so to say, and was clinging to one of the mattresses on the floor I have already
mentioned. Mike had got hold of the top of the open
door of the store closet and was swinging gently to and
fro with it. Jacky had pushed herself down from her corner towards me, and this time we both managed to grab
properly. She clung to me very tightly, and I could feel
her trembling and hear her breathing in deep excited
gasps.

49

"Get me a pair of boots, Steve, for heaven's sake," cried Mac. "There are a couple of spares in the locker too—you can give those to two of the children—they'll be able to tighten the straps up so as to make them fit reasonably well."

With Jacky still round my neck I moved over to the locker for the boots. I gave the Doctor his pair, strapped a pair on Jacky, and handed the third pair to Paul. Mike worked his way down the closet door and we got him across the cabin to a pair of floor-straps. Then we all looked at each other in silence.

"Well!" said the Doctor at length, his face set and grim. "I suppose you children realize what you've done? Have you *any* idea how serious a situation you're in? Do you know where we're going?—to Mars!"

They looked at us with white scared faces.

"We didn't mean it, sir," said Paul tremulously. "Honestly we didn't."

"How did you get in here at all?" asked the Doctor in some exasperation. "That's what I can't understand."

"We were . . . exploring, sir. We saw your rocket in the enclosure up at your house last Sunday, and then we heard of it from old Mr. McIntosh, the gamekeeper, and we—we thought we'd like to have a closer look at it. We didn't mean to do any harm, sir—really we didn't. And we're very sorry if we've upset you."

And then out it all came, the whole story as you already know it—how they arranged to get back from the picnic early, how they got over the stockade wall, how they hid in the store closet when they saw us approaching the *Albatross*.

". . . And, of course, we went unconscious for a time," finished Paul. "And then, when we came round, we went all light-headed. The door must have got jammed in some way, because we couldn't open it for a bit, and we had to knock on it and call to get out. We were floating about in there, and then the door opened suddenly and we floated out."

"You can count yourselves lucky you didn't suffer any worse effects than a bout of harmless unconsciousness from the start-off," grunted the Doctor. "You were young and healthy enough to get off lightly."

He surveyed them sternly.

"And whether we like it or not," he said, "you're with us now. There's no sort of hope of turning back—I can't control the ship properly in empty space going at this speed. My heavens!" he exploded suddenly, "little did I think I'd have three children on this trip with me! Children! You'd think it was a holiday outing to Brighton! And it's a voyage to Mars, do you understand?—the first in history! You're on your way to Mars!"

The children stared at him sheepishly. At least, Paul and Jacqueline did. Mike was behind them, and out of the immediate gaze of the Doctor. And I'll swear he was grinning—and that I heard, as a gentle whisper in the air of the cabin, the one triumphant word—"Whoopee!"

We had calculated before leaving earth—or rather, the Doctor had—that if we achieved through his patent fuel the truly incredible initial speed we hoped for, it would take a little under three weeks for the *Albatross* to reach Mars. As I have said, once we got into outer space, we had no outward notion of time. The Doctor, however, was able, eventually, to calculate day and night by examining the surface of the earth as it came into our view as a globe—he observed the rotation of it on its axis, and from that, allowing for our movement, got a fairly reliable standard of measurement.

As the journey progressed we settled down to a routine —we grew accustomed to the extraordinary conditions. We all kept diaries of sorts—jotted down something at least of our impressions (the Doctor, of course, as well as a personal notebook, kept a most careful and scientific log which has since proved invaluable to astronomers). Writing at first was very difficult—the merest push of a pencil sent it floating off the paper altogether (we had to write with pencils: ink simply would not flow from the nib of a pen). However, this, like everything else, soon came under control. It is a brief selection of some of the most representative entries in these odd journals and notebooks that makes up the next part of this chapter. Here they are:

Dr. *McGillivray's Personal Notebook*—2nd Day. Everything goes according to plan. The ship travels beautifully —to us on it, by a paradox, almost imperceptibly. There is nothing I can do to steer the *Albatross*—we can only pray that I did not in any degree miscalculate our direction when leaving earth, and that we shall fall within the

A Journey Through Space

gravitational pull of Mars. If we do not, then—heaven help us!—we travel from now to the end of time—lost in space—another meteor, no more. Our food (of which, fortunately, I have enough in store for these unhappy children who have joined us)—our food would give out, our air would exhaust itself—we should die here unmourned in measureless space. No one would know. Centuries hence, if we had not collided with a planet or meteor, we should still be traveling on and on, going nowhere—nowhere! . . .

But this is pessimism. Useless to dwell on such thoughts —I cannot have miscalculated. I was too careful—I checked and counter-checked everything. . . .

My days are very full. I make continuous observations —I am well equipped with instruments. The earth is now visible as a vast globe, seemingly over our heads—terrible and beautiful against the darkness of space. Further out, when it is smaller, we shall see it in phases, as it were the moon—in thin crescent and half crescent. It is unbelievably beautiful and fascinating. . . .

Extract from the Journal of Michael Malone—2nd Day of Journey. This is the most wizard thing that has ever happened to anybody, I bet. It's terrific, I can tell you. Of course, we're used to this business of not having any weight by this time, though it wasn't half funny to begin with. There are only two pairs of magnetic boots for us three, so we've got to take it in turns to go into the strap things on the floor. Sometimes, if we feel like it, we have a float around for a lark (ha-ha, but no pun meant—a

53

"lark," see???). It's eating and drinking that's the joke, though. Old Paul had some sandwiches left in his haversack and we had a shot at eating them the first day. Gosh! When you put them up to your mouth they just went floating on out of your hand up to the ceiling! And when Jacky tried taking a drink of lemonade out of a cup, it just came out in a sort of bulb and doddered about in the air—and I had a swipe at it and it didn't burst or anything —it just sort of oozed and crept over my hand like a sort of queer oil. So the Doctor had to show us how to eat and he'd had a really great idea for that. All those things we thought were tubes of tooth-paste in the cupboard where we hid were really food! There were all sorts of things—vegetables like spinach done up very fine, and meat-paste things, and sorts of thick soups, and concentrated essences and whatnot, all shoved into these toothpaste tubes. You take one, you see, and put the point of it in your mouth, and then you just squeeze. You can't chew properly or anything—it just goes into your mouth and then you swallow it (you've got to learn how to swallow with muscle movements, because there isn't any weight in this stuff, see, and it won't go down by itself— but you master that after a time, same as everything else). Drinking's the same sort of idea—the water is in rubber bag things, like hot water bottles, with a tube at the end, and you put the tube in your mouth and just squirt.

The Doc's not so bad now. He was a bit sticky at first about us being here, but he's getting over that. As a matter of fact, I think he's beginning to like us, though he won't admit it yet. He likes explaining things and all that. He's not half a bad stick, really, and I think Uncle Steve's secretly on our side, so it'll be all right. Oh boy, the more I think of it—going to Mars! This'll be something for the chaps at school! Not half it won't!

Stephen MacFarlane's Journal—3rd Day. How can I possibly, possibly describe in any adequate way the wonders that surround us? Sometimes, as I gaze through the port-holes, I find my mind tottering on the edge of things —how can one begin to conceive the incredible vastness of space?

The sky, surrounding us on all sides, presents a new kind of spectacle—a beautiful one, yet a terrible one too. We see, as it were, with an awful clarity (because, the Doctor has explained, light rays are no longer being reflected or obscured by any kind of atmosphere). The whole wide expanse of space is perpetually a deep bluish black, smooth and velvety, yet luminous too, in a strange and totally indescribable way. The stars (unbelievably brilliant) are always visible, yet the sun shines all the time. And how it shines! It is impossible to look at it without powerful dark glasses. When I do look at it so, I perceive that it seems just a little smaller (Mars is further away from the sun than earth, and so as we travel we recede from it).

But it is the spectacle of the earth that haunts and fascinates. At first, as we journeyed, we saw it only mistily —a large, greenish-bluish expanse behind us. Then we came to see the outlines—the whole outlines of countries

55

—and even to be able to observe the huge curve of the surface. Think of it—to see the whole of Britain in outline, as we did, surrounded by the deep blue, sparkling, shining sea!—a gigantic relief map in vivid green, with only the largest rivers traceable as silvery thread-like veins in the body of it, and dark vague blobs for the larger cities—London, Manchester, Birmingham, Glasgow. As we traveled, the country seemed to flatten out and elongate, as it were the reflection of the relief map in a vast distorting mirror. More and more outlines came into sight —France, then the coastline of Spain—Norway. Then—gradually—the whole sweeping curve of the globe; the stark whiteness of the polar caps—the earth as a gargantuan ball, all of it—an enormous shining sphere, filling the whole of space with its radiance, it seemed at first, then slowly, slowly contracting—and all the time, more and more obviously as we receded, revolving on its axis.

Now, on the third day, the earth is about ten times the size of the full moon as we would see it from back home in Pitlochry. It shines with a terrible hard brilliance—silvery, seeming cold. Britain is no longer separately visible—it is no more than a little green finger attached to the vague mass of Europe. Only the bigger shapes are recognizable—America, Africa. The seas are a greyish blue (strange how colors still are visible, despite the brightness of the earth: but they are—only, in a shrill and luminous way). The two poles are pure, pure white—little caps, they seem—skull caps.

As we recede the colors grow less distinguishable. Already the green of the continents is becoming only a gentle tint, and a bright, phosphorescent silvery-whiteness is beginning to flood the whole surface. Smaller land masses are beginning to appear only as vague shadows. . . .

It is awesome and terrible. Yet fascinating—I spend hours at the port-holes, staring and staring. . . .

A letter from Jacqueline Adam to her Mother—written on the 12th Day. My darling Mummy,—It seems such a strange and silly thing to be doing, sitting up here in space, millions and millions of miles away from you, and yet writing a letter as if you were only a few towns away. And, of course, it'll never be delivered, because Doctor Mac has explained that even if I dropped it out of the *Albatross* it wouldn't fall down home the way that maybe you would think it would—it just wouldn't drop at all. It has something to do with there not being any gravity --I don't really understand it, but anyway, that is what Doctor Mac says.

But you see, I'm not really writing to you thinking this letter will ever reach you—it's only a sort of imaginary letter, because I want to put down my thoughts to somebody, and can't speak to you the way I would really like to.

Oh, mummy, I get so frightened! I can't help it, and I try not to show it, but I do all the same. And there is no one to turn to—not even Uncle Steve, though I am sure he understands inside the way I am feeling. It is so terribly lonely out here, although there are the five of us, and we are all quite cheery. But it is not that—it is a different kind of loneliness—not the loneliness of not having people. When I look at the earth (and it is very tiny now—not so big as the moon—just a sort of large star), I think of you there on it, and Aunt Marian, and old Mrs. Delaware next door, and the milk-boy, and the little red mail box at the corner of the street. And it is all very queer and far away and like a dream, and I can't help crying a little bit inside for it all being so lost and strange. You see, it is all so terrible and so big and so cold-looking here, and it is always the same—always, always, always. And I think of things like you and Paul and me on the sands at Bournemouth, or the little cottage in Cornwall last year, and old Mrs. Tregerthen, do you remember, and the strange way she talked, and bathing in the sea, and going down the old tin mine—and Tibby, her cat that had only one eye and was lame in one leg. Oh mummy!

But it won't be long—the Doctor says it won't be long. And we shall all be back again. And you will be better by that time, and we shall be able to sit round the fire and have toast and roast chestnuts (Mrs. Duthie in Scotland was showing me how to make soda scones on a "girdle," and Scotch pancakes, so I shall make some of those for us in the winter, and we shall have them hot with butter).

I shall never forget all this—never, never, never. But secretly I shall never want to come again, no matter how wonderful it may be on Mars. The boys are wonderful —Mike is enjoying himself no end, and so is Paul, but I think that sometimes in his bones Paul is a little bit

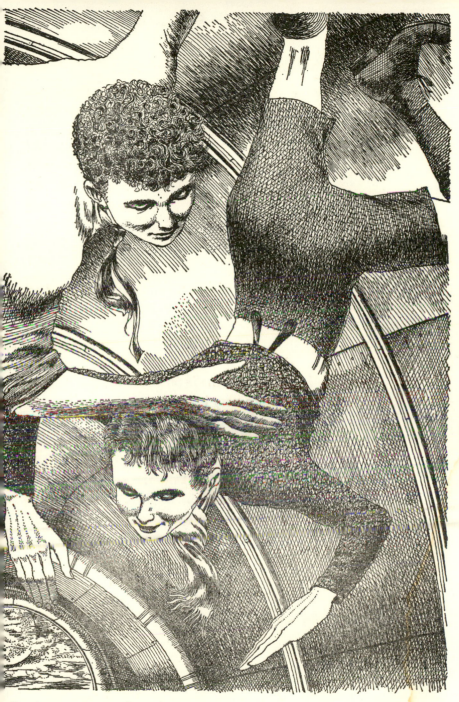

floating game near the ceiling

worried about us, because he is the oldest, lest anything should happen to us, and then he would feel responsible.

Well, this is silly. But it has done me good to write it all down. Perhaps we shall never come back—oh mummy, I couldn't bear it! Well, I won't think of it, that's all.

Mike and Paul are having a floating game up near the ceiling, so I shall go and join them and that will cheer me up. I am sure the Doctor likes us now—he was angry at first, but that is all past. He is a darling, very gentle and kind.

Good-bye for now, darling mummy. I think of you all the time, and so does Paul, I know, in his heart. Get well soon. All, all my love. Your affectionate daughter, Jacqueline. . . .

A Note by Paul Adam made on the 16th Day. A week ago we saw Mars as a very big star. It has got larger and larger. Now it is almost the size of the moon on a clear night on earth. We are almost there!

We are terribly excited. We can hardly believe it. Doctor Mac says there is no danger now of missing the gravity belt—we shall land on Mars—we shall be the first human beings from earth to land on Mars!

We wonder and wonder what we shall find. Will the air be breathable? Will there be food? Will there be water? Will there be people?

We crowd to the port-holes and stare all the time. To think we have actually done it! We have actually done it! . . .

A Journey Through Space

So I end the quotations from our notebooks. The journey was fantastic, beautiful. The conditions on it were such that no human beings had ever experienced before. Yet so adaptable is man, that after the first few days we accepted those conditions as normal. There was no mystery any more—we grew accustomed to weightlessness—we grew accustomed to taking our turns of sleep strapped to the beds—to eating—to everything. So that, towards the end, we were even—yes, I must say it, in all honesty—a little bored and tired, and anxious for the long, long journey to end.

Our minds were full of speculation. As we neared our goal—the red planet—the Angry Planet, as I had referred to it so many days before in Scotland—we talked among ourselves endlessly, imagining, dreaming. At first, as we approached, the planet appeared to the naked eye as a small red disc. As it got larger, we gradually perceived vague dark outlines. There were, as on earth, two polar caps—unmistakably—and therefore, to our joy, moisture on this new world of ours—and an atmosphere.

Nearer and nearer. We could see, revolving in the sky round the planet, its two satellites—its twin moons. The shapes on the surface resolved themselves. There were large reddish patches now, tinted and luminous, as the earth had been. And then, vaguely at first, a creeping green. The globe grew larger—grew immense. And, unmistakably, the outlines of countries—of countries!—came into view. The green patches spread and changed in color to a steely blue—they were, we saw, huge seas. And the red patches—which changed to orange and then to a strange mottled brown—were vast land masses. They were enormous—bigger than even America and Asia had seemed on earth at a similar distance.

There are no words to describe the Doctor's excitement when he was able to announce to us that we were entering the planet's gravity belt and falling rapidly towards it. There was no question at first of any cessation of the sense of weightlessness, for we still traveled faster than the gravity pull on Mars. But he warned us that as we entered the atmosphere, and he set in motion the rocket motors in the front and sides of the *Albatross* to impede our fall, we would experience a return of the terrible pressure we had felt on leaving earth—but not, he believed, so powerfully, since Mars was so much smaller than our own home planet, and the gravity pull weaker.

In my mind, as I look back now, the impressions of the last few hours of our journey are muddled and confused. We were all, I think, a little hysterical—I remember we laughed and chatted inordinately—we talked the wildest nonsense, we hugged each other and danced stupidly and clumsily in our magnetic boots. The shining surface of Mars grew enormous—it filled the whole space beneath us. We were still many thousands of miles from it—there was no hope of distinguishing any detail in the vast land masses below. All we could see, before we entered the outer stratosphere, and so were enveloped in the milky mist we had seen on first leaving earth, was that the seas were after all comparatively small, and that they extended, as it seemed, symmetrically, in broad well-cut channels towards the two poles. The whole center part beneath us was land—there was no danger that we should fall in water.

I saw the Doctor adjust his breathing mask. He stood now, in a sort of icy calm, at the control panel. I and the children lay down on the mattresses, strapping ourselves down. (We had given the other breathing mask to Jacky, so that things would be as comfortable for her as possible.) There was, among us, an awed, incredulous silence.

The Doctor pressed a switch. There was a long quivering tremor throughout the *Albatross*. The motors in the nose were working—we were slowing down. In a moment or two the Doctor would touch the lever that would cause to shoot out the two stocky wings on the back of the *Albatross* near the nose. So the ship, mechanically adjusted for this part of the flight, would flatten out automatically in a long steep dive, so as to land right side up. The Doctor's calculations were such that if there were a brief spell of unconsciousness for the travelers in the last stages of the journey, the tremendous deceleration would slow the *Albatross* sufficiently for the body to adjust itself before the last few miles had been traversed. Thus the operator would have recovered, and be able to work the control panel for a comfortable landing.

There came now, suddenly, in our ears, a high-pitched persistent rushing sound. And gradually our sense of weight returned. I felt myself swimming in the head—there was a repeat of the sensation that someone had bound my chest with iron chains. I looked at Mike, beside me, and at Paul and Jacky on the other mattress. The two boys were white and sick-looking, fighting for breath. I looked at the Doctor. He still stood at the control panel, but he was gripping the hand-rail tightly and swaying a little. He, because of his mask (he wore it as a slight measure to keep himself conscious for the landing) was experiencing the awful weight sensation rather less than we were. The last thing I saw before my senses left me altogether, under the terrible pressure and the maddening rushing sound that filled my ears, was the unsteady, wavering movement of his hand as he raised it to touch one of the controls. . . .

I came to myself gradually, swimming up through blackness. I felt slightly sick. I lay for a moment perfectly still, collecting my powers. Then, as a sort of icy shock, I realized that the darkness was not only in my head—the whole cabin was dark—not pitch dark, but full of a grey, heavy twilight.

"Mac," I cried, "what is it? What's wrong—for heaven's sake, what's wrong?"

And his voice came back, cheerful and reassuring:

"Steve—Steve—don't worry. Don't you realize, man—it's only night—we're landing in the night-time!"

"I'll put on the emergency light," I called to him. "The switch is just above my head here."

"No, don't do that," his voice came. "I can see quite well—I didn't go completely unconscious—only hazy, and my eyes are used to it—it isn't fully dark, it's only twilight. If you put on the light you'll dazzle me. Are the children all right?"

There came two faint reassuring voices from the other

mattress—Jacky, like the Doctor, had taken off her mask before the rest of us had fully regained consciousness. Mike, beside me, grunted and said: "Yes—sure we are."

"Splendid. We're almost there. You can unstrap yourselves and stand up—you'll be able to do it without boots. We're coasting quite slowly—the atmosphere must be fairly dense."

We stood up. Our eyes were accustomed to the gloom by this time, and we stared at each other's vague shapes. I raised my arm. It seemed curiously heavy for a moment, after the long, long spell of weightlessness we had gone through. I had unstrapped my boots before lying down, and now I made a few tentative steps across the cabin. To my joy I found I was walking normally—clumsily, but normally. I saw the children moving, too—we were ourselves again.

And now the Doctor said:

"Are you ready? I'm going to land her. As far as I can see it's flat beneath—I've been coasting round in a circle to make sure, and there aren't any obstacles—trees or anything. There'll probably be a slight bump, so look out."

He was as happy as a king. This was his moment—all that he had worked and waited for.

We stood perfectly still, clinging to the handrails. For a moment there was silence, then suddenly a chuckle from Mac. And simultaneously a heavy jar and a shudder along the whole ship. We pitched forward involuntarily—I heard a little yelp of pain from Mike as his head bumped the wall.

And then all was still. We had arrived!

65

"Ladies and gentlemen," cried Mac, "or rather, lady and gentlemen—our grand tour of the universe is at an end! Allow me to present to you the new British holiday resort—the planet Mars! Tickets, please!"

He roared with laughter. Then, like a schoolboy, he waltzed lightly over to the door of the cabin. He opened it. Before he opened the outer door he looked round at us—we could just see him in the dim light.

"I'll test the atmosphere first," he said, "to see if it's breathable."

He put on his oxygen mask again. Then he closed the inner door. We all stood silent in a little group in the center of the cabin. We heard the outer door open. There was a moment's suspense, then the inner door opened again and Mac once more confronted us—without his mask!

"Perfect!" he cried, "the veriest ozone!"

With whoops of joy, all our excitement released at last in one glorious burst, we rushed to the cabin door. A breeze—a wonderful, soft, cool breeze of real air, thin and sharp, like a perfect poem of a wine—an actual breeze blew in our faces!

We crowded the doorway, staring out. All round us was the twilight. Through it, and immediately in front of us, was the dim outline of what seemed to be a small hill. And above it, streaking the sky, was a brightening tinge of luminous pink.

The Doctor whistled suddenly through his teeth. And when he spoke his voice was different—was quiet and awesome.

66

"Oh my heavens," he said. "Steve—children—do you realize what it is? It's the dawn! It's the Martian dawn! We have arrived at dawn—could anything be more magnificently significant! We're on Mars—and it's the dawn!"

We stared at each other. And I felt my heart swelling inside me, and a lump in my throat from sheer pride and thankfulness after all we had gone through.

"It's the dawn," I repeated softly. "We're on Mars, and it's the dawn! . . ."

CHAPTER V. JACQUELINE ADAM ON "A MARTIAN LANDSCAPE—FIRST IMPRESSIONS"

(*Editor's Note:* This contribution was originally written as a free-subject school essay by J.A. when she returned to normal life on earth. It was later, as an interesting curiosity, printed in the annual school magazine.

It is inserted here in the present volume because this seems the natural place for it—it fills very appropriately a gap in the various papers that Stephen MacFarlane left for me to edit (I should say, incidentally, that there are several such gaps in MacFarlane's collection; the papers were passed to me before they were properly completed and annotated, though the children's contributions had all been corrected for spelling and punctuation).

The essay, may I add, is reprinted from "The Wellingborough Magazine," No. 23, Vol. 5, by kind permission of

the Headmistress of the Wellingborough Hill High School
for Girls, Dorset.—J.K.C.)

MY COMPANIONS and I effected our landing
on the planet Mars in the early morning. It was, indeed,
dawn when we first set eyes on our "brave new world,"
to quote the Immortal Bard of Avon.

There were five of us: myself, my brother P—, our
cousin M—, Mr. McF—, and the leader of the party,
Dr. McG—.

We were naturally curious to see what our new home
looked like, but from our position in the doorway of our
space-ship, we could at first see little. We were, as far
as we could judge in the dim morning twilight, lying in
a small depression, or saucer, surrounded by a high ridge.
(I hesitate to call it a hill—it was only slightly taller than
our rocket).

Our first impulse was to lower the ladder and rush to
explore, but Dr. McG— gave it as his opinion that it
would be better to wait till full daylight before venturing
out. We had no idea of what we might find on Mars, and
he felt it safer for us to be able at least to see any danger
that might assail us.

We were constrained, therefore, to remain in the rocket
till, if I may quote the late Poet of Empire, "the dawn
came up like thunder." I must confess that the simile in
this instance is not a very suitable one. The dawn, as it
came, was somewhat mild and gentle. There was a deep
pinkening of the sky first, which presently spread all

round our small horizon. This changed soon to a deep orange color, and then, to our joy, we saw the thin smoky edge of the disc of the sun rise slowly above the ridge confronting us. The twilight dispersed, and in about half-an-hour the sun—a smaller sun than any I have ever seen on earth—was riding in a clear blue sky.

Our first Martian day had begun!

We perceived now, on examining the ground beneath us, that we were in a dry hollow, the floor and sides of which seemed to consist of a dark brown, reddish earth, or sand. There was no sign of any vegetation—the ground seemed curiously barren and dead to our eyes. Dr. McG— ventured the opinion that it was probably volcanic.

We prepared to leave the rocket. Dr. McG— opened a locker and took out some firearms. He handed Mr. McF— a large rifle and took another such for himself. He also strapped a pistol round his own wrist and handed a second small pistol to my brother. P—, I may say, greeted this gesture with no small pleasure.

The flexible steel ladder was now lowered, and one by one we descended it. Our joy at standing once more on *terra firma* can better be imagined than described. The *terra* in question was, we could perceive on closer examination, a reddish, coarse-grained species of sand, very dry and loose; it was on the question of its being *firma* that we received our first Martian surprise.

We were standing in a group at the foot of the ladder. I may say, that in descending, I had experienced a strange lightness—a sensation of buoyancy. I attributed this at the time to excitement and pleasure combining to fill me with elation. It seemed, however, that the cause was altogether more physical.

M— was the first of the party to move. He gave a cry and jumped forward, intending to rush to the top of the declivity facing us. In a moment, however, and after one step, he was rolling on the ground a good ten feet away from us, his face a perfect study of dismay and bewilderment!

P— rushed to his aid, and he, too, seemed to stumble, and go rolling and bouncing over the sand. Before either of them could rise, Dr. McG—burst into hearty laughter.

"Of course," he cried, "I forgot! The force of gravity—it is not so powerful on Mars as it is on earth. I should have warned you!"

And he went on to explain something of the mechanics of our situation. I regret I cannot reproduce his statement with any real technical exactitude. But as far as I understood things, this was the position. (I am able to quote some actual figures since I made notes of them in my diary):

The planet Mars is considerably smaller than our own earth—its diameter, indeed, is very little more than half that of our mother planet. Nor is it so dense—if the density of earth be represented by the unit 1, then the density of Mars is about .72. For these reasons, the gravitational pull on the surface of Mars is not so strong as the gravitational pull on the surface of the earth—the actual ratio is something like .38. This means that a man weighing say 150 lb. on earth would, on Mars, weigh only 57 lb.

Reflect now that our muscular development is such as

to provide us with the means of moving ourselves on earth in what is to us a normal way. On Mars, where we weighed little more than one third of what we did on earth, our muscles seemed abnormally developed.

While Dr. McG— was engaged in this explanation, the two boys had succeeded in raising themselves to their feet. M—, full of excitement, now exclaimed that he proposed doing a "high jump." We knew him, on earth, for a reasonably good jumper. Judge now of our surprise when we saw him soar into the air, high above our heads! P— immediately also indulged in a short "flight," and soon we were all at it—yes, even the two more sedate members of the party! The sensation was quite indescribable. I myself, at the school sports last year, cleared the four foot bar; with the same effort here on Mars, I found myself soaring into the empyrean a good ten feet! It was like pole vaulting without the pole—and the landing was soft and pleasant. There was no heavy jolt—a gentle bump on the yielding red sand and that was all.

It was exhilarating in the extreme. After the long period of confinement in the cabin of our space-ship, the exercise in the rare thin atmosphere did us all the good in the world. Even running was an excitement—an ordinary earth-pace covered eight or nine feet. It was like walking in seven-league boots, as Tom Thumb did in the fairy tale. We hopped about in our little hollow like kangaroos, shouting merrily in the sunshine and generally behaving like lunatics.

Presently, however, the first novelty wore off. We set about trying to control our muscular movements so that

What we saw was awe-inspiring and strange

we might be able to walk as we were accustomed. And we found that, just as we had been able to adjust ourselves in space, when we had no weight at all, so we could, after a little practice, adjust ourselves to moving about comfortably on Mars. We could still, of course, if we wanted to, make prodigious leaps, but for the most part we contented ourselves with the more ordinary mode of progression to which we were used.

The time had now come for us to widen our field of exploration. The sun was high and the air was clear. So Dr. McG— assembled us at the foot of the ridge and we set about mounting to the top of it (an easy task this, because of our reduced weight, although the slope was quite steep—indeed, almost vertical).

We reached the summit. And now, indeed, we felt like "stout Cortez, when with eagle eyes," etc. (Keats). Only our peak was on Mars, and not in Darien. However, what we saw was just as awe-inspiring and strange to us as the glimpse of the far Pacific was to the intrepid Spaniard.

Before us, bright and silent in the sun, was a huge plain. It stretched, as far as we could immediately judge, some eight or ten miles before it was terminated by a line of high bare mountains. They—as indeed was the whole plain—were of the same reddish color as the soil in our hollow. Every now and again, in the surface of the plain, as we could see from the incline on which we stood, there were similar deep hollows to the one in which our spaceship lay, behind us.

But what gave the scene its character, what caused us the real wonder, was the vegetation. Dotted all over the plain were immense clumps of huge, dark green, leathery plants. It is impossible to describe them other than very generally, since each individual plant varied in shape from its neighbor. Some of them were tall—as tall as good-sized church steeples—others were small and squat, mere bulbous masses clinging to the ground.

The nearest large clump of these plants was about five hundred yards away in front of us, and since it was quite clear to Dr. McG— that there was no immediate danger threatening, we set off at once to conduct a closer examination, using our leaping ability to cover the ground quickly.

I have said that the plants were dark green in color. That is the effect a clump of them created at a distance. But seeing them at close hand, we observed that many of the individual plants—particularly the smaller ones—were mottled with large irregular patches of yellow, and even (in some of the very small bulbous ones) dark red—a somewhat evil coloration, this, without brilliance; somber and heavy, like coagulating blood.

I have said that the shape of the plants varied individually, and this was indeed so. But one feature they all had in common: they were composed of short squat stalks with huge finger-like leaves on them. These leaves were convoluted into fantastic shapes—like twisted vast fingers sometimes, with rheumatic joints, seeming to grope up into the air as if stretching and grasping after the sun.

The nearest I have seen on earth to these strange and evil-looking Martian plants are the *cacti* in the Botanical Gardens at Kew. But the Martian species was smooth and more leathery—and presented, moreover, a much richer variety of shapes, besides a wider range of color.

Dr. McG— was considerably excited as we stood surveying the plants.

"It means," he said, "that there is water somewhere—or at least moisture of a sort. When we were standing on the knoll back there, I looked all over the plain for some sign of a stream or a lake, but there was nothing. Yet moisture there *must* be, or these huge things simply could not exist."

As he spoke, he took out a long sharp knife he carried in a sheath at his waist. He advanced to one of the plants that was about man-size and stabbed the knife into it, at the point where the short stalk branched out into the leaves. There was a soft, unpleasant squelching sound, and simultaneously it was as if I heard in my head—hardly in my ears—a high-pitched wail or scream, as if from an immense distance.

I looked at my companions. Their faces wore a puzzled, listening expression.

"Did you hear anything?" asked Mr. McF—.

"Yes," I vouchsafed. "It was a kind of scream. Yet I can hardly say that I *heard* it. It was rather as if I . . . well . . . *thought* it!"

"That is what it seemed to me too," nodded P—. "It must have been imagination—there is nothing within miles that could possible have made that sort of noise. But it's strange we all heard it at the same time, though."

While we spoke Dr. McG— was stooping forward examining the deep triangular gash he had made in the

76

leathery flesh of the plant. A milky, viscid fluid was oozing out of it, and simultaneously an acrid but not unpleasant odor assailed our nostrils. Dr. McG— touched the sticky-looking gum with his finger and conveyed some of it to the tip of his tongue. For a moment he frowned, as if trying to assess the taste, then he nodded his head.

"M'm, quite nice," he said. "Like sweet butter-milk, almost. Rather sickly, I should fancy, if you took a lot of it. Well, moisture there undoubtedly is, as I have said before. To judge from the dryness of the soil, it must be very far down. I should guess that these things have immensely long tubular roots. I propose to come back with an axe and a spade to cut down one of the bigger ones to make a thorough examination. Meantime, I must confess that I am getting very hungry—this keen air has whetted my appetite considerably, and in all the excitement of the landing we have quite forgotten to eat. I have some food in the refrigerator back in the rocket—we may find, later on, that these plants are edible, but meantime some real earth-quality bacon and eggs would not come at all amiss after so many weeks of tooth-paste food, eh?"

We greeted this suggestion with great acclaim, and immediately set off back to the hollow where we had left the rocket. On top of the ridge we turned and looked once more at the strange and desolate landscape spread out before us. There are no words to describe the extraordinary bare silence and stillness of it—yet I had the impression, as I looked again across the enormous poisonous-looking dark green clumps to the mountains, that there was something, *something* disturbing the silence. No sound—nothing as definite as a sound, although it seemed a sort of sound: again it was as if I were *thinking* it, rather than *hearing* it. A vague rustling disturbance—a sensation of disquiet vibrating all about us.

I dismissed the feeling as mere fancy and descended the ridge with the others. Soon all else was forgotten in our excited arrangements for what was to be our first real cooked meal since leaving earth.

That, then, was our first glimpse of a Martian scene. I conclude by saying in all humility that I am only too aware of the inadequacy of my poor pen to describe the strangeness of it. I console myself with the reflection that the intention has been there even if the performance has been weak—"a poor thing, but mine own," to draw once more in quotation from the teeming works of that great figure who towers as a mountain above the plain of literature: William Shakespeare.

(*Note:* The rest of this chapter consists of disjointed comments by Stephen MacFarlane. It is evident, I think, that he originally intended writing a long chapter here on the reactions of the party on first landing on Mars—he has even, as you will see, completed some parts of it, particularly the closing paragraphs. But for some reason he left this part of the book to the last—at no other point in the whole collection of papers is there such a gap.

I will explain later how it was that the papers came into my hands before MacFarlane could polish them. Meantime, as matter of interest, I print his notes for this chapter exactly as he left them.—J.K.C.)

"A Martian Landscape"

MacFarlane's Notes:

General coverage of Chap. 5: first impressions; experiments in jumping (possible dissertation by Mac on gravitational differences between earth and Mars?—Mac also on subject of composition of soil in hollow where we landed?)

We climb to top of ridge. General excitement and reaction to landscape, etc., etc. Describe curious plants and so on. Work in a couple of paragraphs about distant hills —something along these lines:—

While Mike and the others were talking about the curious plants in front of us, I was surveying the distant hills through my binoculars. It was clear from a first examination of the plain that there was no sort of human life on it. I was, in my own mind, positive that there was life on Mars—why should there not be?—we were plainly alive and comfortable on the planet: the air was breathable: there was, as the presence of the plants showed, moisture. So I searched the hills through my powerful lenses to see what traces of habitation there might be there.

The hills were barren. They seemed, as far as I could see, to consist of huge porous red rocks—rather like sandstone as we know it on earth. I seemed to perceive, on the lower slopes, patches of green—possibly, I thought, mountain varieties of the plants immediately in front of us. Only once did I have any impression that I might be looking at something connected with human life. Just as I was lowering the binoculars from my eyes, I saw, behind

79

the shoulder of one of the lower hills, a sudden brilliant flash. My first impression was that the sun was reflecting from a hill lake, but I soon saw that this was impossible— the flash was half-way up the hill, and seemed, as far as I could see, a sort of crescent—not lying horizontally, as a lake would, but at an angle along the hill-slope. I swept the glasses along the range to see if there might be any other such flashes, but there was nothing; and when I moved them back to the original spot, the bright crescent had gone. It had not been in my field of vision long enough for me to be able to form any real opinion as to what it had been.

Description of plants at close quarters—write up in some detail. Extraordinary episode of far-off screaming noise, *seemingly in our heads*, as Mac cut into one of them. What can it have been? Plainly nothing immediately near us that could have caused it—*except the plant itself!*

A bizarre, extravagant notion—but in a sense the only one that offers any real explanation. Could it *possibly* be so? Write up whole theory at some length.

Various remarks—conversations, etc., as we move back to the *Albatross*. The party in excellent spirits—Mike enjoying his high-jumping hugely. Various points mentioned by Mac—his intention to take some photographs of the scene etc. Work in this way towards end of chapter. End chapter thus:—

. . . and within a very short time, the boys had the

"A Martian Landscape"

Primus working (how extraordinary to see such a homely thing as a *Primus* here on Mars, with all its associations of picnics and alfresco outings of all sorts on earth!), and Jacky was busying herself with cooking the bacon and eggs that Mac fetched for her from the refrigerator. Soon, drifting out on the thin sharp air, there came the delicious smell of real, freshly-cooked food—real food, after all our weeks of vitamin pastes and sieved vegetables! Mike turned a good half-dozen huge cartwheels in sheer ravenous excitement.

Jacky insisted that we did things properly, and so we set out a clean bed-sheet as a tablecloth. There were not enough plates, knives, forks, and so on, to go round (after all, we had reckoned on only two travelers in the *Albatross*), but since the food had to be cooked piece-meal in our one small frying-pan anyway, that did not worry us a great deal—we took our viands in turns. When the meal was eventually over, we sighed deeply and contentedly and lay back in the sand—which was now quite warm from the sun. I lit a pipe and passed my tobacco pouch over to the Doctor.

"Well, Mac," I said, smiling, "we're here. We've made it, after all. I don't mind confessing to you now, that in the old days back on earth, I often had my doubts—I thought sometimes that maybe your lab assistants were right and you were just a little bit mad!"

"To tell you the truth, I thought so myself at times," he said with a warm chuckle.

So we puffed contentedly in the sunshine, watching the fumes of the Virginian tobacco, grown so many millions of miles away, go drifting lazily up to disperse in the clear air. I felt deeply satisfied with myself—one of the very first human beings to land on Mars! Think of it—I, Stephen MacFarlane, a writer of books, a weaver of dreams, creator (in my head) of fantastic adventures! . . . and here I was, actually engaged in the flesh in an adventure more wild and fantastic than any I could *possibly* imagine!

As I lay there in the sun, relaxed and comfortable, I felt a curious drowsiness coming over me. After all, it was a long time since any of us had slept properly, in all the excitement of the landing. Perhaps the fresh strong air had something to do with it too, and the fact that we had just had a large meal—a meal that gave our digestive organs rather more work than they had had for a long time. At any rate, it was all I could do to keep my eyes open. I looked round at the others. Apparently they were being affected in the same way; Paul and Jacky were already actually asleep, and Mike was not far from it. Mac's pipe had fallen on his chest and he was making no effort to retrieve it. He smiled at me lazily.

"Feeling sleepy, Steve, eh?"

I nodded.

"No harm in having forty winks, I suppose."

"None at all." And he yawned. "I'm certainly going to —I feel incredibly drowsy—the excitement, I guess."

I sighed and yawned myself, and then closed my eyes and settled myself to doze.

I slept deeply—we all did, as I afterwards learned. I remember—and it comes back to me with a curious distinctness, even after all this time—that I had a vivid and vaguely terrifying dream, about the huge dark green plants we had just been examining. It was as if I were walking down an immense avenue, bordered by two endless rows of them; and as I walked, on and on, there was a whispering and rustling among them, and then, slowly —almost imperceptibly—they began to stoop down towards me. Lower and lower they came, and now the rustling changed to a high-pitched faroff screaming, very faint and eerie. I started to run, but the avenue was endless. And now the plants were very low and very near— their huge fleshy fingers were reaching out to grasp at me. I had a knife in my hand, and I hacked and stabbed at the great leathery writhing fronds—and with every stroke the screaming grew more and more intense.

I became aware of someone shaking me violently by the shoulder. I opened my eyes drowsily, and Mike's face swam into my consciousness. Mike's face—but it was strained and anxious.

"Uncle Steve," he was saying urgently, "Uncle Steve, wake up! Look—for the love of Pete, just look!"

I sat up abruptly, on the instant wide awake, so insistent had been Mike's command. The others were awake too, and staring, just as I was.

And well might we stare! On the ridge above us, standing silently gazing in at us, were creatures!—creatures vastly, vastly different from anything that any of us had ever known, but living creatures—individuals—Martians!

And as I stared at the tallest of them—the one plainly their leader—I heard him address us. And the language was English—English!

For a moment I thought I must still be in my dream. But the sun was shining, my companions were all about me. They, as plainly as I, heard the cool, detached, faroff tones:

"Who are you? Who are you? What are you doing here?"

CHAPTER VI. THE NARRATIVE CON-
TINUED, BY STEPHEN MacFAR-
LANE: THE MEN OF MARS

WE ROSE to our feet. Jacky moved over towards me, and I put my hand on her shoulder to allay her nervousness. We were all nervous. Why should we not be?—there was something unutterably awesome in the very quietness and immobility of the two-score odd creatures above and all around us. How long had they been standing there, gazing down at us while we slept? The vast plain had been empty—now, from nowhere seemingly, these beings had appeared, creeping unerringly to the one hollow among all the hollows in that expanse that held a secret.

What did they look like?—what was our first impression of them? It is difficult to say. Since that first day, I have known them so intimately, have studied them at such close quarters, that I can hardly remember how they *first* seemed to present themselves.

There was nothing, in the whole range of our experience of living beings on earth, to which they could quite be compared, although in general shape they were not unlike human beings. They were small, varying in height from 4 to 5 feet—their leader, to whom I have already referred as the tallest, was about 5 feet 6 inches. Their bodies were slender, smooth and round; in general dimensions comparable to the trunk of a medium-sized silver birch on earth. In color they were, in general, yellowish—a dark, patchy yellow ochre; but this deepened to green towards the foot in most cases, and sometimes merged to a fleshy pink and even red at the top. At the top, this trunk of theirs, as I have called it, bulbed out slightly into a head (I am, in this description, forced to use analogous human terms—"head," "trunk," "hands," and so on; but, as you will see later, the Martians are quite different from us—the words are used only as *equivalents*, for the purpose of building up some sort of image, however imperfect, in your minds). This "head" was covered, on the rounded top, with a sudden fringe—a sort of crown—of small soft tufts of a vivid bright yellow color. Just below this, on the front—the "face" (although strictly speaking the Martians, as we decided later, had no faces—or rather, their faces were these tufts or crowns on the top that I have described)—there were three, sometimes four, sometimes even five, small jellyish bulbs—

glaucous protuberances which glowed transparently. These were the eyes. There were no organs of hearing or smell —at least, in that first glimpse we could see nothing that might be an ear or a nose; we found out later, as we shall describe, that the Martians had a very highly-developed sense of smell, although they could only "hear" sounds of considerable loudness.

I now come to describe the "feet" and "hands" of the Martians. At the lower extremity of the trunk—the greenish part I have mentioned—the body suddenly bifurcated. Each of the forks split again almost immediately, and so on and so on, so that on the ground, at the foot of each figure, there was a perfect writhing mass of small, hard, fibrous tentacles. About a third of the way up the trunk, in the front, there was another sudden branching of similar "tendrils," as I might call them—only these ones were longer and lighter in color and seemingly more sensitive. These were obviously the "hands," since they held, in their twining grasp, the Martian weapons—long spears, or swords, of some bright transparent crystalline substance —a sort of flinty glass, as it seemed. Finally, to complete this sketch of the appearance of the Martians, there were, just under the bulb of the head, and on each side of the trunk, two smaller clusters of tentacles (or "tendrils," as I really prefer to call them). These were very short and slender, and light green, almost white in color—like small pale sea anemones.

These, then, were the creatures that confronted us that first morning on Mars. The task of describing them properly has been almost impossible—as I say, I have had to use human terms—we think, us men, almost always in terms of ourselves ("anthropomorphically," as Mac would say—a monstrous big word meaning, quite simply, just that—thinking of everything, the whole universe, in terms of ourselves, as being *like* ourselves). The Martians were quite, quite different from ourselves—it was not till we grasped that that we began to understand them. As our story goes on, and you begin to learn more about these strange creatures of another planet, perhaps you will be able to form a clearer picture of them than I have been able to give in the brief sketch above.

The thing that astonished and unnerved us most, however, at that first meeting with the Martians, was not so much their appearance, strange as that was. It was the fact that the leader was addressing us, and that the language he was using was our own English, as I have said already at the end of the previous chapter.

"Who are you?" he said distinctly. "Who are you? What are you doing here?"

I looked wildly at Mac—it seemed, at any incomprehensible moment of our whole adventure, the only thing to do; he was the wisest of our party—a Doctor of Philosophy, no less; if anything was understandable, he surely could understand it—if he did not, what chance had we?

Mac, alone among us, seemed to have recovered some of his composure. He looked up at the leader of the Martians and said, in a clear slow voice:

"We are men. We come from earth."

There was a rustling round the top of the ridge—a mercurial quivering of those hundreds of white, wormy tendrils. And the response came immediately—seemingly from several of the Martians at the same time—in the chill, detached tones:

"What are men? What is earth? Explain, explain, explain. Who are you? Where do you come from? What are you doing here?"

The terrifying thing was that I could not see anything in the way of a mouth on the creatures. How were they talking at all, let alone talking in English? Where was the sound coming from? And yet I knew, in my bones, that there *was* no sound—that I was not *hearing* what the Martians said! The sensation was exactly the same as that that we had experienced when Mac cut into the huge cactus-like plant on the plain, and a scream seemed to come *into our heads*. I remembered what Jacky had said on that occasion—it was as if we were *thinking* the sound rather than hearing it. Now it was as if I were *thinking* these cold, detached, insistent questions—they were forming of their own accord in my brain! It was an uncanny experience—it was impossible not to feel uncomfortable and a little terrified. Jacky shivered at my side—I could see that the boys' faces were pale and strained.

"Mac," I cried, "for heaven's sake what is it? How are they speaking to us?—how in the Lord's name can they be speaking to us?"

He was curiously calm—when I look back I always think of this as Mac's best moment throughout our whole adventure. He was, on earth, a quiet, reticent, scholarly man—the last man to possess, in any marked degree, courage as we have come to define it. But courage he did have

—courage within his own terms of reference: the courage of brains, of sheer intellect—he confronted the incomprehensible with his own weapons, his *brains*. And he was confident in the possession of those weapons, and in their efficiency—he was confident and cool in the face of this strange enigma now, standing with one hand loosely on the pistol at his belt, the other raised to shade his eyes from the sun as he gazed up at the Martian leader.

Without shifting this gaze for a moment, he now answered me.

"I don't know, Steve," he said quietly. "I do have a glimmering notion—no more than that yet. Give me time —just a little longer."

Then he raised his voice again, and addressed the Martian in the same loud clear tones as before.

"Before I explain further who we are," he cried, "tell me who you are."

Again the rustling and the quivering, and again the response:

"We are the Beautiful People."

Quick as a flash, Mac turned round to us.

"Tell me, Steve—what did they say?" he asked.

"Why—'We are the Beautiful People,'" I answered dazedly.

"And you, Jacqueline—tell me what you heard them saying."

"I thought they said—'We are the Lovely Ones,'" said Jacky timidly.

"Ah! And you, Paul?"

"I agree with Jacky," said Paul.

90

"So do I," volunteered Mike. "That's what I heard them say—'We are the Lovely Ones.'"

Mac smiled.

"Steve," he cried, "I believe I've got it. Watch this— I'm going to ask them a question—I'm going to ask them if they knew we were here or if they came on us accidentally. *And you won't hear me saying a word.* Watch."

There was a silence while he gazed up at the Martian leader, with a curiously tense expression on his face. Presently there was the usual quivering among the Martians, and there floated into my head:

"Yes. We knew you were here. We were told. We had a message."

"I was right, Steve!" cried Mac immediately, to me. "I know what it is! Try it yourself—look at that big fellow, the leader—ask him a question. But don't say anything— *think* it to him, in your head—think it as hard as you can —put all your powers of concentration into it."

I did as he told me. I stared at the Martian leader and thought, in my head:

"How did you know we were here? Who gave you the message?"

There was no quiver—no response.

"You're not thinking hard enough, Steve—you're probably a bit nervous," said Mac. "Make an effort—*throw* your thought towards him."

I tried to calm myself, and repeated the mental question with more concentration. And this time the response came back:

"We were told by our friends the Plants, whom you injured."

I stared at Mac helplessly—the whole thing was too much for me. Apart from the uncanny business of the conversations, this latest response—that the Plants had told the Martians of our presence—was bizarre and incredible. But Mac, far from seeming as baffled as I was, was actually smiling triumphantly.

"Steve, it's magnificent!" he cried. "Who would ever have thought it! It's so simple, man—don't you understand?—it's *thought transference!* It isn't speaking at all, as we understand it—it's pure communication—what scientists back on earth have been arguing about and experimenting with for years. These creatures have got it highly developed—they can plainly communicate with each other by simply thinking a thought and so projecting it. That's how they can speak to us—we receive the thoughts they project—and of course, we receive them in the form we are accustomed to think in—in our case English. I got the final clue when you said you heard them say 'Beautiful People,' while Jacqueline claimed they said 'Lovely Ones.' You were both right—the thought is the same in both cases. 'Lovely' is probably a word that Jacqueline and the boys use more frequently than 'Beautiful,' which is a literary word, natural to a writer like you. If a Frenchman had been with us, he would have claimed that the Martian said: 'Nous sommes les Beaux.' If my old rival Kalkenbrenner were here (and I bet he wishes he was!) he would have heard the thought in his own native language of German: 'Wir sind die Schoenen Leute.' It's the

92

pure thought we receive—we translate it in our heads into whatever language or form of language we're accustomed to."

"But, Mac," I protested, "it's fantastic—it's unholy! Does that mean they're listening-in now up there to all this conversation of ours—these ideas that are flying to and fro between us in the form of language?"

"I doubt it," he replied. "I think we may take it that the thought has to be consciously projected in a certain direction—otherwise we would have known that the plants out there were busy summoning the Martians to our hollow here."

"Do you mean that the plants have it too—this power?" I gasped.

"Undoubtedly. You heard what he said—or rather, what he thought at us. Probably they only have it in a primitive way—they could only transmit thoughts of danger, say, or fear—they couldn't express any coherent thought to us, for example, because they have not got coherent thought. But a message that strangers were among them—a possible source of danger—such a simple thought could be passed from clump to clump till it reached our friends up there and summoned them."

I was beginning to understand.

"And that scream we heard—it was the plant after all?"

Mac nodded.

"A really intense thought like that—a protest against pain—that would 'get over' because it's simple enough for the plant to direct, even to such imperfect receivers as us. My dear Steve, it's beautiful—it's perfect and beautiful in its sheer simplicity and economy! Language is a clumsy thing—half the trouble in the world arises from people not understanding each other because language expresses thought so imperfectly. These creatures don't have to use a clumsy tool like language—they can exchange *pure ideas!*—think of it—sheer thought!"

He was excited again. In the glow of a scientific discovery he seemed totally oblivious to our situation. As far as I was concerned, I had the drift of what it was all about—I did not understand in detail yet, but I realized at least that communication with the Martians was possible, and that the thing to do now was to establish friendly relations with them, and go into the whys and wherefores later.

I looked up at the creatures on the ridge. Throughout the whole long conversation between Mac and me they had not moved—they still stood staring down at us quietly. One of the most disconcerting things about them (I found it so even later, when I knew them better) was this gift of theirs of complete immobility.

I addressed the leader, putting all my concentration into the thought I was projecting.

"We are friends," I said (for convenience's sake I shall use words like "said," "replied," etc., in reporting our conversations—our exchanges of thought, rather). "We do not mean any harm to you."

And, rather surprisingly, the response came:

"We know. If there had been evil intention in you we would have felt it at the first when you looked at us. But you have not yet explained. Who are you? You are not like us. Where do you come from?"

I was puzzling in my mind how this question could possibly be answered simply and satisfactorily, when Mac said to me:

"It's no use, Steve—we can't explain anything as complicated as that at this stage: we shall have to wait to find out how much these creatures know of the universe—there will have to be some common ground of knowledge before we can exchange thoughts about the earth and so on. Leave it to me for the moment—I've got a suggestion to make to them. I might as well speak aloud—that gets the thought over just as well, and it means we all know what is being said."

He turned to the Martian leader and addressed him in these words:

"Where we come from and who we are are difficult things to say. We shall be able to tell you in time, when we know you better, and when you know us better. What we would like to do now is to go with you to see the rest of the Beautiful People—you know we are friends, and so we want to see you and the places where you live. Will you let us come?"

There was a short pause, then the rustling and quivering again. This, we learned later, was all we could perceive of thoughts being exchanged among the Martians —a vague disturbance in the atmosphere, as it were. Finally the leader said to us:

"Yes. You can come. We shall welcome you as our

friends. And we shall hear in time who you are and what you do among us."

"Good," said Mac. Then he pointed to himself and added:

"I am McGillivray. That," pointing to me, "is Mac-Farlane. That is Jacqueline, that is Paul, and that is Michael."

At this there was a disturbance—Mike plainly was overcoming his sense of awe and strangeness, and was almost himself again, for he said now, in some indignation:

"It isn't Michael—I hate Michael! It's Mike!"

The leader extended the long crystalline spear he held in his front tendrils and gravely pointed it at each of us in turn.

"McGillivray—MacFarlane—Jacqueline—Paul——"

He hesitated for a moment.

"Mike," cried my redoubtable nephew fiercely.

"Mike."

Then he gestured with the spear to himself, and we heard, clearly and slowly in our heads:

"I am Malu—I am Malu the Tall, War Prince and Counsellor of the Beautiful People."

And in some way this seemed to set the seal on this, our first encounter with the Martians. Our nervousness went—even Jacky confessed that she no longer was afraid, only timid and (her own word) "shy." We mounted into the rocket to fetch some necessities—some tins of food, lest, as the Doctor explained, we should find nothing edible among the Martians. We also took some water, some coats and blankets, cameras, and a small compact recording equipment the Doctor had brought from earth. It was easy for us to carry all these things, we found, because of the reduced weight they had on Mars.

Thus laden, we descended the ladder, Mac taking care to lock the door of the *Albatross* behind us. We climbed the slope and confronted Malu—Malu the Tall, who was barely a foot bigger than Mike! And so, surrounded by the strange and silent, but no longer sinister Beautiful People, we set out on our second Martian journey of exploration—Mike occasionally, as he gained confidence, leaping high into the air, even laden as he was, just to show what he could do.

Appendix to Chapter VI *by Dr. McGillivray.* Mr. MacFarlane has suggested I should add a footnote to this chapter by way of amplifying his remarks on thought transference. There is little I can say: I consider that he has given a reasonable, balanced and clear account in the preceding pages of how we first learned to communicate with the Martians (an account somewhat flattering to myself, albeit: I deserve no credit for what was, after all, a simple process of deductive ratiocination, wedded to the type of instinctive perception a scientist is almost bound, by his training to acquire). It occurs to me, however, that it might be relevant for me to make a few parenthetical remarks on the subject of thought transference as we know it on earth.

It has been believed for a long time that there are good scientific grounds for assuming that such a thing as thought transference—telepathy, as it has been called—

is possible. We all know the simple, almost everyday experience of suddenly thinking of something at the same time as someone else—very frequently two people, apropos of nothing, will start on the same sentence together in a conversation. Even allowing for coincidence, the number of well-authenticated cases of this sort is such as to suggest that thought occasionally can be transferred direct from one mind to another.

Unfortunately, in the past, telepathy has been allied to such doubtful subjects as clairvoyance and second sight —even fortune telling—and so has got surrounded by a mass of superstitious beliefs, legends, and exaggerations, thus precluding the possibility of a proper assessment of its validity. However, towards the end of the last century, several unbiased scientific minds set to work to examine impartially the arguments for and against. Unfortunately, although some extraordinary experiments were conducted, and remarkable results obtained, at that time there were not enough operatives involved for the findings to be considered general in application—moreover, the experiments, it was considered, were not conducted in such a way as to rule out *all* chances either of coincidence or deliberate fraud.

Not long ago, however, a group of workers allied to and subsidized by an American University, set about tackling the subject in an absolutely true scientific way. They collected first a great mass of evidence for telepathy and sifted it to the roots. They then devised a series of very simple and fool-proof experiments. These consisted of preparing a set of cards, like playing cards, with certain clearly printed symbols on them—a circle on one, a square on another, a cross on a third, and so on. There were five such clearly differentiated symbols, and ten cards to each symbol—thus fifty cards to a pack.

Two people are now arranged—say in separate rooms —so that they have no obvious way of communicating with each other. One or them *thinks* to the other a certain symbol, and the recipient chooses a card from the pack. Now it follows that since the number of symbols is known, and the recurrence of each symbol in the pack is known, the *mathematical law of averages* can be used to calculate the number of times when the right card would be chosen by *sheer chance*. A regular score of "right guesses" above that number would seem to suggest—even to the most sceptical and impartial scientific mind—that the card-choosing subject is being controlled by the symbol-thinking subject: and if this score goes on through a vast number of experiments—each one carefully checked and notated by detached observers—then it can fairly be assumed that thought is being transferred from one mind to another.

This is a sketchy description of only one of the experiments that have been conducted over a considerable number of years—are, indeed, at the time of writing, still going on. After a vast amount of research, and the ruthless rejection of anything not 100 per cent proven, the scientific group to which I have referred are of the opinion that *there is definitely such a thing as thought transference*.

So far, on earth, no real success in deliberately transferring coherent ideas has been achieved—experiments have been confined to simple things like symbols on cards. On Mars, as we have seen, thought transference of a very highly-developed type is the normal means of communication. It seems obvious that because of their evolution along these lines, the Martians have developed super-efficient transmitting and receiving faculties—hence their ability to communicate with minds like ours not normally adapted to this mode of converse. It is significant that we humans on Mars, although we grew expert in communicating with the Martians, were quite unable to communicate by means of thought transference with each other. We frequently tried projecting thought among ourselves in the same way as we did to Malu and his companions, but always without success. In the end, we got into the habit simply of speaking to the Martians aloud. This meant that we humans understood what was going on, and the thought behind the speech still got over as *thought* to the Martians.

As far as the ability the Martians seemed to possess of being able to understand the elementary thought processes of the plants is concerned, I hope to be permitted to contribute to this volume at a later stage a paper setting forth my own theories as to what the Martians were—theories that may seem outrageous, but which you may be prepared to accept when you have heard more about the general mode of life on our sister planet from the gifted pens of the other writers of this book.

I hope these few notes may help to make clear and acceptable to sceptical minds Mr. MacFarlane's remarks in the previous pages.

CHAPTER VII. FIRST SIGNS OF AN ENEMY, BY PAUL ADAM

IT'S MY turn again to do a chapter, but to tell you the truth I'm not very confident about this one. There's so much about the Martians and their city and so on to describe at this point, and I'm not really awfully good at description. However, for the sake of not letting Uncle Steve down, I'll have a shot at it—and anyway, I'll get Mike to do an occasional paragraph, just to help out. So here goes.

Well, now, I'll start at the point where we left the good old *Albatross* to go with Malu and his friends to see the rest of the Beautiful People (that's what we've all decided to call them in this book, though as you know, Jacky and Mike and I really thought at the beginning that they were called the Lovely Ones). The first thing

I want to say is that those Martians could certainly move at some speed when they tried. Uncle Steve has described their feet—sort of forking tentacles or tendrils (by the way, I've got to hand it to Uncle Steve for his description of the B.P. in the last chapter—considering how difficult it is to give anyone a clear idea of what Malu and Co. looked like without just sounding crazy, I think he's done marvelously). Well, when they're getting about, the Martians move these hundreds of tentacle things one after the other at a great rate—it looks like a quick sort of flailing movement at a little distance. And when they do this they simply scoot across the sand, whipping up little clouds of it as they go. It's really a most curious sight—their bodies stay quite upright and still, you see, so that it looks as if they were on wheels.

As far as we were concerned, well, we had no difficulty in keeping up a pretty good pace ourselves. Walking and running were dead easy on Mars, because of the lower pull of gravity and all that sort of thing. Each step was worth about three on earth, so we could go at a reasonable, easy trot and cover the ground in no time—and it wasn't in the least bit tiring either.

As we went (we were making for the hills on the other side of the plain, by the way), Doctor Mac was having a conversation with Malu. I don't quite know what they were saying, because we were a little bit behind, but I think the Doc was trying to explain something about us and where we came from and so on. Anyway, you'll learn all about that sort of thing later on: the Doc has got another chapter all about his conversations with the Martians. I'm only concerned with the actual adventure part of what happened to us.

Jacky and Mike and myself were speeding along right in the middle of the Martians (Uncle Steve was in front with the Doc). Curiously enough, although I suppose there was a lot we could talk about, we hardly said a word. Somehow the Martians didn't seem very communicative, and after all you must admit that it was a bit shy-making being with such odd creatures. We weren't frightened in the least—it's very difficult to describe, but we didn't *feel* that the B.P. would do us any harm—there was no sort of distrust or suspicion at all. I suppose this *feeling* of things had something to do with the business of thought and so on being transferred. On Mars you always knew if anyone meant harm before they even spoke—you didn't have to rely on things like facial expressions and so on. Actually, the Martians didn't have any facial expressions—they never changed at all in appearance. If they were happy about something, then you just *knew* it—you felt it in your bones, sort of thing. And if they were miserable or afraid, then you knew that too, although there wasn't the slightest bit of difference in the way they looked.

Anyway, as I say, we felt a bit shy and strange during the journey. Very occasionally Mike had a shot at saying a word or two, but that was really all that happened till we got to their city.

Insert by Michael Malone: There was one quite small Martian traveling alongside me and I thought I'd have a shot at drawing him out a bit. So I said sort of chattily after a time:

"We're children, you know."

There didn't come any answer (I found out later that this Martian's name was Nuna, by the way—they mostly had short names like that). So I said:

"Don't you know what children are? Not grown—the same as Mr. MacFarlane and Dr. McGillivray, only not so big or old. Young, you know—aren't there any young Beautiful People?—before they grow as big as you?" (It seemed a bit comical to be saying this, because Nuna wasn't any bigger than me.)

Anyway, this time the answer came back:

"Yes—there are young among the Beautiful People. You shall see the young. They do not move."

"Gosh," I said. "Don't move?—that must be awkward. How do you mean don't move?"

"It is not possible to explain," said Nuna. "You shall see, and then you will understand."

It was a bit of a whack in the eye, this, but anyway I waited for a bit and then I said:

"Don't they go to school or anything?"

"What is school?" says Nuna.

Well, there wasn't any easy answer I could think up to that, so I just left it there.

Well, that's all I've got to say at the minute. I thought I'd chime in here while old Paul was writing about our journey from the *Albatross*. I'll leave it to him now to carry on for a bit. Here he goes:

104

First Signs of An Enemy

At the rate we were traveling, it took us a little under an hour to reach the hills (a distance of some nine or ten miles, we reckoned). As we approached the lower slopes we saw that growing on them there were trees—unmistakably trees. They were taller than most earth trees, although the trunks were quite slender (the wood was very hard and strong, we discovered later, yet quite light). Where they differed most from our trees was in the leaves: these were large and bulbous, with dark green spikes at the ends of them. Doctor Mac told us later that the thick fleshy quality of the plants on Mars was probably due to the very dry nature of the soil. It was necessary for them to store moisture in their leaves—sort of vegetable camels, you know.

We plunged into a thickish forest of these trees and started to climb. During this part of the journey we were aware of a sort of tension among the Martians—a curious vague sense of danger, and of being on the alert against it. The flank members of the group raised their long crystal lances and kept them pointed outwards.

However, nothing happened. And presently we burst clear of the trees. We had, during our ascent through them, rounded the shoulder of one of the hills, and now we were on a kind of plateau, looking down on a wide shallow valley. And in it—well, here is where I've got to make a shot at a bit of description, and as I've said I don't consider myself very good at it. However, here goes.

Below us, spread out on the floor of the valley, were about forty or fifty huge domes of what looked like glass —at any rate, a transparent substance of that nature. They

were huge—gigantic oval humps, or bubbles, sparkling in
the sun. They were of varying sizes. The smallest, I should
say, was about the size of the dome of St. Paul's Cathe-
dral: the largest—which was right in the middle of the
valley, towering above all the rest—covered an area easily
as large as Olympia in London. In color the glass was a
mild sea-green, though in one or two of the smaller domes
there were long streaks of milky blue.

Inside these domes, and also moving about on the
ground all round and between them, we could see hundreds and thousands of the Beautiful People. As we descended from the plateau and moved towards the domes,
scores of them formed in lines to stare at us with those
queer fishy eyes of theirs. And at closer quarters like this
we saw that many of them were smaller than Malu and
Co., and of a different color, being a very light and pleasant yellow, merging to a gentle pink at the top. In these
smaller ones, too, the crown on the top of the head was
much larger—sometimes quite six inches tall—and much
more brilliant in color. We even saw one or two that were
a flaming, very lovely scarlet. These smaller Martians, we
found out later on, were the females. Malu and Co. were
males, though, being apparently the picked warriors of
this particular group of the B.P., they were taller even
than most of the males.

Malu led us through the crowds and past several of the
great glass domes until we reached the big dome in the
center. Here we stopped for a moment while Malu went
into a sort of tunnel entrance just outside the wall of the
dome. Through the glass we could see him reappear from

a similar tunnel entrance inside and move forward among the crowds of B.P. inside the dome.

We put down our various bundles and waited.

"How do you feel, you children?" asked Uncle Steve.

"I feel fine, personally," said Mike. "Boy, this is wizard! I never expected anything like this!"

"Nor did I," chuckled Uncle Steve. "I remember back on earth, before we set out, saying something about life on Mars, if there was any at all, being different from life as we knew it. But I never thought it would be different in quite this way."

"Do they know we come from earth?" asked Jacky. "Were you able to explain, Doctor Mac?"

"Partly," said Doctor Mac. "I think our friend Malu understands roughly what it's all about—the Martians do have some sort of knowledge of the universe, apparently, and I was able to get one or two general ideas over to him. But he's a soldier, as he said. He's going to take me to their Wiser Ones, as he calls them—I expect that means their scientists."

"Is that where he's off to now?" I asked.

"No. He's gone in to what he calls The Center—we've to meet The Center first, whatever that is. And then the rest—these Wiser Ones—have to be summoned by what he calls The Voice."

"It's these houses I can't get over," said Jacky. "At least, I suppose they are houses. They're huge! How could they ever *make* them?"

"That's just one of the many things we'll learn as time goes on," said Uncle Steve. "I must admit they are a bit of a mystery—there aren't any frameworks to them, as far as I can see—just huge bubbles. It must have been the sun shining on one of these that I saw through my binoculars this morning."

We were still talking along these lines, surrounded by a big staring crowd of the Martians, when Malu came back through the tunnel entrance.

"You are to come," he said. "You are to follow me to The Center."

So now it was our turn to go through the tunnel. It was quite short—a slight slope down and a slight slope up. And then we were inside the glass dome.

Seen from the inside, it was enormous—a huge huge tent all over us. The glass was not so transparent as it seemed, for there was quite a twilight inside—not dark, but at least the bright sunlight was diffused. But the odd thing was that it was so warm inside the dome—there was a kind of oppressive clammy heat, rather damp and steamy; it was like one of the milder hot-air chambers in a Turkish Bath my father once took me to in London.

There were crowds of the Beautiful People inside the dome, most of them males, though this lot were quite considerably smaller and rather paler in color than the Malu bunch—they were sickly-looking and somehow a little repulsive. They were standing in lines converging on the center of the huge dome, and we advanced, led by Malu, through a lane of them.

Presently we stopped before a closely-packed wall of the B.P.—bigger ones again, of the Malu type.

Malu turned to face us. Then he said:

"The Center."

—and stood to one side.

Immediately the wall of Martians parted, and we saw, before us, on a heaped-up mound of the red sand, the biggest Martian we had yet encountered. He was not particularly tall—only very slightly taller than Malu; but somehow there was an impression of a sort of vastness about him. His trunk, shorter than Malu's, was very thick —as thick as an oak-tree on earth. It was his head that gave the real impression of size, though—it was an enormous pinkish bulb. And it was surmounted by a crown rather like Malu's round the edges—yellowish and tufty— but mounting towards the center to a huge cockscomb— a brilliant waving plume of deep poppy-red. The little bunches of tendrils on each side of the "face" were longer than usual, and they seemed all the time to be wavering slightly in the air. The "face" itself was very strange. It was somehow almost transparent, and its substance did not seem as fleshy as on the other Martians. It was kind of soft and jellyish, and it too seemed all the time to be quivering slightly—a sort of pulsation, it was, just under the surface.

This being—The Center—lay at an angle on the little mound I have mentioned. For a time he stared at us with his bulbous, luminous eyes (there were four of them), and then he said:

"Which one is the leader—McGillivray?"

The Doc stepped forward. There was a long long silence while The Center looked at him. The Doc stood perfectly still and straight. At length The Center said:

"You and your friends are welcome among us. What you are, we do not know. You are different from us—much different. We have never seen creatures like you. You will explain what you are and where you come from, to me and to the Wiser Ones when The Voice has summoned them. We know you do not mean evil, and that you have interesting things to say. So you will be cared for and protected. You will let us know of anything you require, and it shall be provided if it is in our power to provide it."

Doctor Mac bowed. Before he could say anything, the solid wall of Martians had closed up again in front of The Center. Malu moved forward, and we realized that our interview was at an end. We followed Malu to the tunnel, and so found ourselves out in the open air again—which seemed, by the bye, very pleasant and refreshing after the stuffiness of the dome.

Well now, where do I go from here? There's so much to write about—that first day was so crowded—that I hardly know where to begin. Besides, I don't want to poach on Doctor Mac's territory—I know he's got a lot to say about the Martians (he has a most interesting theory about them, by the way), and he has a chapter coming along soon. I think I'll just leave it to him—he'll be able to make a much better job of it all than I ever could. I'll just deal very sketchily with one or two of the main things that happened, and then jump straight on to when the excitement began (that doesn't mean to say we didn't find it *all* exciting—it sure was; but a different kind of excitement came along early the second morning, when Mike got himself mixed up with—however, that's anticipating, and all the books on writing say that that isn't allowed).

When we came out of the dome we found a little group of the Martians—including Mike's pal Nuna—gathered round our baggage examining the various things. Nuna had picked up a movie-camera in his front tendrils, and was poking about at the various controls. Two females—Malu introduced them (if that's the expression for being made to know names in that queer thinking way) as Lalla and Dilli—they were feeling over a blanket. As best as we could we explained what the things were for, but it really was surprisingly difficult. The idea of "blanket" they just managed to get, but the camera was quite beyond them, and so were the tins of food and the guns. We decided that we would have to wait a bit, till we got to know the Martians better and what (to quote the Doc) their "ideological background" was, before we could hope to get over the more complicated sort of ideas.

The next thing that happened, after we had got our stuff together again and packed on our backs, was that Malu and Nuna led us through the city to one of the domes on the edge of the valley. They told us that we could make this our headquarters. We went in through a small tunnel and dumped our stuff in a clear space that Malu indicated not far from the inner entrance. (The dome, by the way, was quite full of Martians, standing quietly in little groups—it was really an amazing sight;

all they did when we went in was to turn and stare at us with those queer eyes of theirs—they didn't seem to show any surprise—they weren't half as curious as a bunch of earth-folk would have been, say, if some Martians had suddenly appeared among *them*. We found out later on that everybody in the city had been told about us, by means of all this quick thought transference business, from the first moment we arrived; and we also found out later, as we got to know them, that the Martians were not terribly curious about things—they liked to have things explained, certainly, but they never *pressed* for an explanation; and if they never got one at all, well, it didn't seem to worry them in the slightest—they just accepted things in the most curious indifferent sort of way.)

The first thing we wanted to know about was food—it would be awkward if we could not find anything edible on Mars. Besides, we wanted to know how the Martians ate and drank, not having any mouths, you know. We managed to convey this idea to Malu, and he led us out of the dome and across to a part of the city where there was an immense clearing. Here we saw a most curious sight.

In this clearing, or field, there were, growing in orderly lines, hundreds and thousands of the cactus-type plants. They were much smaller than the ones we had seen on the plain, and lighter in color altogether. The leaves, too, were not so leathery. Moving among these plants were some hundreds of Martians. Every now and then, one of them would stop before a plant and lean his head down towards it; then he would stay quite motionless for about four or five minutes. When we moved closer we saw what was happening. Uncle Steve has described the little pendulous feelers, or tendrils, on each side of the Martian "face." Well, the Martians were pressing these things against the leaves of the plants. They were, we discovered, *feeding* through them!—sucking the sap into themselves through the little tentacles! Somehow it wasn't a very pleasant sight at first, although we soon got used to it. (This incidentally, is one of the things Doctor Mac will be writing about later—I only mention it here because it was one of the interesting sights we saw that first day.)

The problem was, what were we going to eat? There was the chance, of course, that we might find the flesh of the plants quite edible, but somehow we didn't like the idea of trying it. We knew that the Martians had a sort of thought transference thing working between themselves and the plants, and the notion of our cutting off leaves and so on—well, it was all a bit nasty—particularly when we remembered how we had heard the scream of pain from the plant on the plain. Strange that on earth we had never thought it might actually be painful for a plant to be cut—grass, for instance. Well, I don't suppose for a moment it can hurt earth plants—come to think of it, they haven't any nerve cells. But here on Mars it was altogether a different matter.

Finally the Doctor had a brainwave. He asked Malu about the trees—did they have any communication with them? Malu said no, so the Doc said that later on we would go up to the forest and gather some of the big spikes and leaves. He would analyze them—he had some equipment for doing so—and then he'd be able to let us know whether we'd be able to eat them or not, and just how nourishing they would be. Meantime, we had enough food in tins not to have to worry for a day or two.

Well, on we went, exploring one thing after another through the city. We took endless photographs, and the Doc, as far as I could see, filled up several notebooks with jottings about this and that. So did Uncle Steve—I expect that as this book goes on you'll get to know, from one or other of them, some of the hundreds of interesting things we saw. I can't hope to cover even a hundredth of the ground.

Insert by Michael Malone: I was keen to get to know about this children business I'd asked old Nuna about before. But all he did was to say the same as he'd said on the plain—that they weren't able to move, and all that. So I said, what about seeing them sort of thing? But he said, well later on sort of—they actually weren't in the city at all. He said we'd go tomorrow into the hills to see them. So I had to leave it at that. Anyway, there were so many things to have a look at that first day that it went out of my mind after a bit. There was one thing that was pretty exciting, I must say. We saw some Martians playing a kind of game at one place, and it was actually a sort of football! Yes—really—no kidding. The ball was a roundish block of wood from one of the trees. They made a big sort of circle in the sand, and there was a shallow hole in the middle of it, see. Then there were some Martians round the hole, and other Martians in a ring outside. And these outside ones had to get the ball through the inside ones and put it in the hole. The way they played was to get the ball caught up in their big sort of tendril things they had for feet, and then they'd scoot along, pushing it as they went. And the defenders would tackle them, see, and try to get the block of wood into *their* tendrils. Sometimes you'd see two of them standing absolutely still together, with their tendrils sort of inter-locked. You thought they were just being matey, maybe, they were so quiet, but all the time they'd be pushing at each other's tendrils with terrific strength—and as I say they were usually so evenly matched that you didn't think they were moving at all. Then one of them would give in suddenly, and the other would career off with the ball until another of the B.P. tackled him in his turn. The real object of the game was this sort of all-in tendril wrestling, apparently—the block of wood was really just an excuse for them to try their strength this way. It was great fun—I'd have joined in, only, of course, I didn't have any tendrils—ordinary dribbling wouldn't have been much use.

I just thought I'd put in this bit about the football here, while Paul is chewing the end of his pen wondering what to say next. I see he's ready now, so I'll pass over to him again and he can carry on.

By this time the day was wearing on (Paul Adam writing). We went back to the dome where our kit was. Somehow we didn't fancy the idea of spending the night in the dome—the atmosphere was too hot and stuffy. We were just wondering what to do about it when Malu, who had gone off for a moment, came back to say that the Wiser Ones were with The Center now, and would the Doctor go to see them.

While he was gone we had a conference. We were beginning to feel peckish again, and rather sleepy (there must have been something in the air of Mars—we all felt very sleepy there). So we opened some tins and had a meal, while a group of the B.P., with Lalla and Dilli well to the fore, stood silently looking at us. The sun by now was nearing the horizon. Suddenly Mike did his famous brow-slapping act.

"I've got it!" he yelled. "We'll build a tent! We can easily rig up a lean-to with a couple of blankets and the rifles—we could borrow some of these glass spear things, too, for poles."

It was a great idea, and we set to with a will. Before very long we had quite a satisfactory little tent erected, and just as the sun was disappearing we crawled into it and made ourselves comfortable with the remainder of the blankets. We had taken a glance into the dome before settling down, to see how the Martians slept. It was very odd—they weren't lying down or anything; they just stood in rows, with their feet-tendrils buried in the sand, absolutely motionless—they might have been so many posts.

Mike was already asleep and snoring when the Doc came back.

"This is a good idea," he said, as he crawled into the tent beside us. "I don't think I could have stood the heat in the dome—I've just been closeted with The Center for the past hour-and-a-half, and the atmosphere was really unbearable. Phew!"

"Did you manage to get anywhere with the Wiser Ones?" asked Uncle Steve sleepily.

"Yes—we got on famously together," said the Doc. "It's been a remarkable experience, Steve—quite remarkable. I'll tell you all about it in the morning. The Wiser Ones are astonishing—really astonishing. I've never known anything like it. By heaven, what a tale it all is to tell when we get back! What a tale!"

"If we ever do get back!" said Uncle Steve. Then he grunted and turned over, and in a few minutes I heard his breathing deepen as he went to sleep.

For a time I heard the Doc crawling about getting ready for bed, but eventually he too settled down, with a long contented sigh, and all was quiet.

Although I was so tired, it was quite a time before I could get to sleep—the strangeness, I suppose, and all the excitement we had gone through. I lay on my back, with my head cupped in my hands, looking out under the edge of our tent. There had been a very short twilight—now it was quite dark (the Doc, by the way, had explained to us earlier that the Martian day and night were almost the same as ours—the cycle lasted about twenty-four-and-a-half hours and not twenty-four—that was really the only difference). The strangest thing to me, as I lay there, was to see two moons overhead—two small, shining moons, very pretty and brilliant against the blue-black velvety sky. The night was clear, and there were millions of stars, in constellations strange to me. One of those stars, I thought

117

(which one I did not know—perhaps that small, slowly-winking one just above the horizon)—one of them was our earth—our home. All those millions and millions of miles away were the things we knew and the places we knew—yes, and the people we knew: old Mrs. Duthie, who had been so kind to us—Mr. McIntosh the game-keeper, with the fish-hooks in his Sherlock Holmes hat—our own mother and father, and Mike's mother and father. It was a strange thought—and a sad one too. They would be worrying about us—perhaps they would have given us up for lost altogether by this time. They might have had search parties out in the hills round Pitlochry. . . . I remember feeling a lump in my throat just before I dropped into sleep—and wishing too that there might be some way, *some* way by means of which we could communicate with them all, just to let them know that we were well and happy.

Well, there wasn't a way. I fell asleep at last, with Jacky curled up beside me with her head resting on my shoulder. All was quiet—terribly quiet. I thought of the strange silent Martians all around us, standing so erect in their big bubble-like houses. The Beautiful People, they called themselves . . . and they were, I could see, a beautiful people: not to look at—we found them too strange to look at yet to be able to think of them as beautiful in that way—but somehow they were beautiful *in themselves.* They were sort of simple, somehow, and innocent. Oh, I don't know. I don't really know what I'm trying to say. This is only what Mrs. Duthie would call "havers" —"blethering." And Mike would call it "sissy talk." Well, perhaps it is; but it's somehow what I honestly felt in my heart at the end of that first strange day of ours on Mars. . . .

I woke suddenly. The light was streaming into the tent. All round me there was excitement and activity. Uncle Steve and the Doctor were up already, completely dressed, and Malu was with them too, together with Nuna and all the Martians that had been with them when they found us—the warriors, the picked men.

"What's the matter?" I cried. "Is anything wrong?"

"Nothing that need worry you," called back Uncle Steve. "We're going out on an expedition, that's all. We won't be long."

"Where are you going?" (This from Mike, who had sprung to his feet and was rapidly buttoning the clothes he had loosened before going to sleep.)

"Nowhere in particular. Just out—into the forest."

"I don't believe you," said Mike. "What are you checking up on the ammunition in that rifle for if it's only into the forest? There's something in the wind, Uncle Steve— you needn't think you can kid us."

Uncle Steve came nearer. His face, we could see, was very serious.

"Listen, children," he said, "Malu has just brought us a message—from the plants outside, in the plain. There's —well . . . there's danger."

"It's the *Albatross!*" cried Jacky. "Uncle Steve—it's the *Albatross!* Something's happened to it!"

"Yes, Jacky, it's the *Albatross*," said Uncle Steve gravely.

"Nothing's happened to it yet, but it may do. That's what we're going out to prevent."

"And we're coming with you," I cried.

"No, Paul—you can't—you children must stay here. The danger is too great."

"But what *is* the danger?" demanded Mike.

"Listen, Mike—I know very little more than you do. But apparently there are, here on Mars, other things besides the Beautiful People. The Doctor heard about them last night from The Center, and Malu has been telling me about them this morning. I don't know what they look like. All I do know is that these things are evil and beastly—they're the deadly enemies of everything in this city. Malu calls them the Terrible Ones—and at this minute a group of them—a small foraging party—is at the *Albatross*."

There was silence for a moment. Then Mike said, in quite a different kind of voice, for him—very serious and slow:

"Uncle Steve—whatever you say, we're coming with you. If there's anything threatening the *Albatross*, we have as much right to fight it as you have. Paul has a gun —Doctor Mac gave him one. And as for me—well, I've got one of these!"

As he spoke, he snatched up one of the long crystal spears that we had been using as a tent-pole. Uncle Steve looked at him—at all of us—helplessly. Then he shrugged his shoulders and turned towards the Doctor, who was coming across to us, looking strained and excited.

"Steve, are you ready?" he asked breathlessly. "Man—
we must hurry, we must hurry!"

"I'm ready, Mac," said Uncle Steve.

Five minutes later we were speeding through the forest,
traveling in gigantic leaps as fast as we could go. Across
the plain we went, silently, Malu and the warriors raising
little red clouds with their flailing tendrils. We reached
the hollow where the *Albatross* lay. We quietly, quietly
mounted the ridge. We looked down into the hollow,
our guns and spears grasped firmly, our hearts beating.
And we saw—we saw—

What we saw—what happened—these things are beyond me to describe. I end my chapter here. I leave it to
Uncle Steve to tell you about—

The Fight for the *Albatross*. . . .

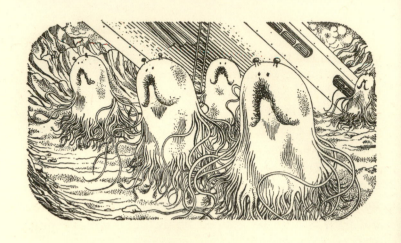

CHAPTER VIII. THE FIGHT FOR THE "ALBATROSS," BY STEPHEN Mac-FARLANE

AS I sit here quietly writing in Pitlochry, with the dark shapes of the hills before me, and above them the star-studded sky, I think of that first encounter of ours with the Terrible Ones on Mars as the one unreal episode in our entire fantastic adventure—unreal, I think, because it was so unutterably horrible—too horrible for one to want to remember it.

What caused the horror? Not altogether the appearance of the Terrible Ones, hideous though that was (the Beautiful People, after all, had accustomed us to strange appearances). No, it was the *silence* in which the battle was fought; there was no sound throughout the entire encounter—no actual *sound*, although our ears were full of a violent, edgy, ghostly screaming all the time. It was impossible to tell who was screaming—friend or foe; it was simply that all about us, through and through us, were running those deep and beastly *thoughts* of conflicts and pain and revenge and death. It was a nightmare—a nightmare in different terms from any nightmare I have ever known, or ever hope to know.

Paul has described how we heard the news that the *Albatross* was in danger early in the morning of our second Martian day, and how we armed ourselves and sped across the plain to the hollow where our space-ship lay. We had half-expected that the enemy, whatever it was, might come to meet us, or would at least be visible as we neared our destination. As it was, however, we crawled right to the top of the ridge without interruption, and were thus able for a few moments to gaze down on the Terrible Ones in the hollow before we were discovered—in much the same way as Malu and his companions had gazed down on us the morning before.

Our first impression was that the *Albatross* was surrounded by gigantic yellow-and-red spotted eggs—or that, in the night, some huge clammy toadstools—fungoids—had formed in the hollow. There was an odd score of the things, pulpy-seeming and glistening in the sunlight, each the size of a small ox. They were moving silently backwards and forwards along the tail part of the rocket (it lay, naturally, on a slope, with the nose high up in the air at an angle), and they seemed, as far as we could judge, to be feeling and nosing at it with long tube-like tentacle things that grew, writhing, out of their sides. One of the creatures had twined his tentacles round the flexible steel ladder, and was swinging it backwards and forwards. They seemed somehow like octopuses—bulbous and jelly-like —with unusually long and slender suckers.

As we stared, two of the things—the two nearest us— turned round in our direction, and it was then that the full hideousness of their appearance broke over us. They had faces! In the front part of their yellow, shell-like coverings there were unmistakable features; two bright protruding eyes—seemingly on short stalks, like crabs' eyes— hard and unblinking, and beneath them two small, nostril-like cavities. But it was the mouth that caused us to grip our rifles more tightly. It was a hugh gash, *vertical* in the face, with great flabby jaws on each side—yellow on the outside, a raw damp red inside. These jaws were held wide open, and the strange thing was that we could not see anything in the nature of a throat-opening inside the mouth, although we were staring full into the great gaping cavity of it. Nor did there seem to be anything resembling teeth; only, lining the inner surface of the jaws, some layers of protuberant lumps that seemed to be, so to say, large taste-buds, as on the human tongue. To complete this brief description, I may say that the egg-like bodies of these monsters were mounted on forking tendrils of the same type as the feet of the Beautiful People.

We had no more than a few moments to take in the appearance of the enemy, for almost immediately after the two nearest us had turned round, there was a sudden cessation of movement at the rocket. One by one the hideous creatures veered slowly to face us—forty-eight hard and unblinking eyes stared up at us. And at the same time I became aware of a terrible sense of evil—there was an atmosphere of sheer malignancy all around us. I realized what it was that Malu had meant by saying earlier that the Beautiful People would have known if we had meant them any harm. By means of the strange Martian telepathy, we were made aware in our very souls that the things in front of us were deadly enemies—they were *thinking* ill to us as we clustered round the ridge-top staring down at them.

For perhaps half-a-minute there was no movement, and then the Doctor acted. He was standing beside me on the ridge, and I knew by looking at his face that he was an angry man. The *Albatross* was his all—and the *Albatross* was in danger from these terrible, evil-meaning things. Sweat stood in little shining drops on his brow as he raised his rifle to his shoulder and fired at the creature that stood at the foot of the steel ladder. What followed was nightmarish.

The Doctor, in his anxiety and excitement, had not paused to aim properly. He had meant to strike between the eyes of the creature. What happened, however, was that immediately on top of the explosion a long deep furrow appeared across the back of the thing by the ladder, as the bullet tore open the flesh of it. There was no blood—only the sudden mysterious gash. And simultaneously, in our heads, a long drawn-out scream of pain and fury. The Doctor fired again, and this time the bullet struck squarely home a little above the nostrils—we saw a sudden hole punched in the face, round and clean. But again no blood. And, to our horror, no seeming harm to the creature! Screaming even more hideously he started to advance across the hollow towards us—they all started to advance, slowly, and in some sort of formation.

"What in the devil's name are they, Steve?" gasped Mac. "You saw me firing—you saw the shots go home! Why doesn't it fall? The Center told me last night about these things, but I had no idea they were anything like this! What are they?"

"Lord knows," I answered grimly. "We're up against something this time, Mac—by heaven we are!"

I looked round wildly at Malu. He and his warriors stood perfectly still—but I saw that they held their long glass swords in readiness before them. Meantime the things below were almost at the foot of the ridge. I wished with all my heart that I had forbidden the three children to come with us. I looked at them as they stood in a little group between Mac and me.

"Paul," I said, "you shouldn't have come! Go back, for heaven's sake—take Jacky back!"

Paul looked doubtfully at his sister—I could see he was a little unnerved, and that, as the eldest, he felt a sense of responsibility, and was inclined to do as I asked. But before he, or any of us, could do or say anything more, Malu and the warriors went into action.

How can I describe the fight that followed?—there is nothing, nothing at all on earth to which I can compare it. We, in our amazement, stayed on the top of the ridge, gazing down as if hypnotized, doing nothing—nothing, that is, until . . . but let me take it all in order.

126

The Fight for the "Albatross"

Malu and the warriors rushed headlong down the slope, their tendrils flailing, their slender yellow bodies upright. About half-way down, twenty or so of the little army stopped suddenly and arranged themselves as a rearguard, as it were—spacing themselves out at intervals, just above the main conflict. Malu and the rest went on, and met the Terrible Ones just at the foot of the slope.

The creature who had been wounded—he seemed to be the leader—was a little in front of the big advancing semi-circle of the enemy. Malu and Nuna both seemed to poise themselves for a moment, and then, with a curious sideways flick of their powerful feet-tendrils, they leaped high into the air straight at him. Nuna came down sideways, close by his flank, and Malu landed barely a foot from his vast red jaws. And as they landed they swung down their crystal swords with terrible force.

Even at the top of the ridge we heard the beastly squelch the weapons made as they sheared through the flesh of the thing. Malu's blow cut an immense gash right across the face—the whole side of the creature's head seemed to fall away; one of the huge jaws and one eye. Nuna took a great slice out of the side—but still there was no blood, only, as the creature heeled over, with his long suckers writhing in agony, a slow oozing white moisture, seeping out over the sand from the two deep wounds. And all the time, growing thinner and more distant in our heads, were the monster's dying screams.

Meantime the other Beautiful People had joined battle with the Terrible Ones, and now it was that the air seemed to be filled with screaming—a jumble and confusion of anger and pain. The attack of the Beautiful People was always the same—a quick upward leap and a deep slash with the sword in falling. Some of the Terrible Ones slithered sideways out of the way of the flashing weapons, and then it was their turn to attack. Their long writhing side-tentacles would shoot out and whip round and round the slender trunk of one of Malu's warriors. The warrior would struggle in the deadly grasp, but once he was caught in this way there seemed little hope for him. Slowly and inexorably his body would be bent back, till suddenly it would snap in two! Then, in an instant, the attacking monster would release his grasp and leave the two halves on the sand, oozing the same sort of milky fluid as the dying leader of the enemy had done, and with the little face tendrils twitching and quivering spasmodically.

All the time, the rearguard of the Beautiful People stood half-way down the slope. Now and again, as an opportunity presented itself, one of them would leap forward with the quick sideways lash of the tendrils I have mentioned, and deal a mighty blow at one of the enemy momentarily off guard. But for the most part they stayed motionless, their long swords outstretched, waiting for one of the enemy to try to climb the ridge. Then they struck, shearing into the pulpy flesh, so that either another monster heeled over in the sand, or staggered back into the melée below, horribly gashed—minus an entire jaw perhaps. There was one startling incident when one of the Terrible Ones rushed precipitately up the slope and impaled himself on a spear before the warrior holding it had time to raise it for a blow. A good two feet of the weapon slid into the monster's soft flesh. For a moment the two antagonists faced each other, motionless, the warrior still clinging to the handle end of the sword with his tendrils. Then the Terrible One made a sudden jerking movement with his whole body. The warrior rose from the ground, hurled into the air in a long arc; and as he fell, further down the slope, the great beastly thing, with the sword still sticking out of his shell, leaped on top of him with a sickening thud. . . .

The battle lasted some ten to fifteen minutes. All the time, we humans stared down, fascinated, longing to help but not knowing how to. Our guns were all we had, and our guns, after the Doctor's experience, seemed useless. Jacky, after the first few minutes, moved back from the ridge, her face pale and drawn. Paul and Mike crouched beside the Doctor and me, Mike, as the fight went on, letting out an occasional yell of encouragement to Malu and the warriors.

Eventually it became obvious that the Terrible Ones were losing ground. Slowly they were being pushed across the floor of the hollow, under the nose of the *Albatross*, the rearguard warriors now joining the Malu group in routing them. As the contestants retreated, the screaming in our heads grew fainter and thinner. Looking down into the part of the hollow immediately beneath us, we saw that eight of the monsters were lying dead under the great gashes that had been dealt them. Five of Malu's warriors had been broken in two, and one of them—the one who had been tossed in the air—had been crushed to death: he was a mere pulpy mass pressed into the sand.

We descended the ridge, Jacky following us timidly. With the cool detachment of the man of science, Mac went down on his hands and knees to examine the remains of one of the great yellow-and-red spotted monsters. He was turning over in his hands one of its huge flabby jaws, when suddenly there was a yell from Mike, and immediately on top of that; the disaster happened.

The way it came about was this: While we were descending the ridge, the battle was still going on on the other side of the hollow. The monsters, realizing they were defeated, were trying to form themselves in some sort of order for a retreat. They were slowly climbing the ridge, hard pressed by Malu and the warriors. One particularly large creature was lingering a little behind, laying about him with his huge suckers to give his companions a chance to get over the top. Malu and Nuna both gathered themselves for one of their deadly leaps—Nuna jumping sideways, Malu towards the jaws. They moved like lightning, but in this instance the monster was too quick for them. He slewed sideways, and in doing so overthrew Nuna. The little Martian's sword bit into the creature's flank, but Nuna himself toppled over and went rolling a little way down the slope. He was able to arrest his progress by digging his tendrils into the sand, but he was plainly a little dazed and could not, for the moment, rise upright. We saw that the huge repulsive creature was gathering himself to throw his vast bulk on top of Nuna to crush him. Malu's sword had carried away part of his

130

ke was swung up into the air, kicking and shouting furiously

jaw, and now the gallant leader of the Beautiful People, realizing, as we did, the plight that Nuna was in, was desperately trying to manœuvre himself for the death leap before the monster could act. But some of the creature's side tentacles shot out and coiled round his waist, keeping him from moving.

Mike had yelled at the moment when Nuna had lost his balance. Now, as the enemy poised himself, he was half-way across the floor of the hollow, moving in gigantic jumps and shouting at the top of his voice. The rest of us gazed for a moment, too astonished by Mike's sudden action to be able to do anything. Then the Doctor shouted:

"Michael—Michael—for heaven's sake come back, boy!"

The flying figure did not pause. All we heard, coming back to us as he took the last few gigantic steps, was:

"It isn't Michael—it's Mike! Whoopee! Hold on, Nuna —I'm coming, I'm coming!"

The action was so quick that we hardly realized what was going on. We ourselves, I should say, were half-way across the hollow by this time, rushing to keep Mike out of danger. We saw him stand for a moment facing the monster, then he jumped high into the air and brought down his glass sword—the one he had snatched from the tent back in the city—across the tentacles that held Malu. In doing so he lost his balance for a second or two, and immediately the creature's remaining tentacles were round his waist, and he was swung up into the air, kicking and shouting furiously. Simultaneously the creature shuffled sideways, flailing at the ground with his feet-tendrils, and in a moment was over the top of the ridge and had disappeared from view, with Mike still a prisoner in the monstrous suckers.

We rushed forward, overtaking Malu and Nuna, who had recovered themselves, and, with the other warriors, were slithering over the top of the ridge. Already the remnant of the enemy force was some hundreds of yards away, Mike's struggling figure held high in the air above them. Shouting insanely we ran after them, the Doctor and I to the fore, Paul and Jacky a little behind. We exerted ourselves to the utmost, taking huge, twelve-feet strides. But the Terrible Ones moved at an extraordinary speed, their tendrils flailing, raising a red cloud as they threaded among the huge clumps of cactus-plants.

The Doctor suddenly stopped. He raised his rifle to his shoulder. But I flung myself sideways and knocked it up in the nick of time, so that he fired harmlessly into the air.

"Don't shoot, Mac!" I cried, "don't shoot! You'll hit Mike. And even if you don't, you know that bullets make no difference to those things."

He lowered the gun and looked at me, his eyes wild.

"Steve," he cried, "what can we do? We can't leave the boy to the mercy of these monsters—we simply can't."

"We'll do whatever we can," I said, trying to sound optimistic, though my heart was full of despair. "We'll have to consult with Malu—these things are too devilishly fast for us."

He nodded. Paul and Jacky had made up on us by this time. Jacky was crying, Paul was white, with quivering

133

lips. Presently Malu and Nuna joined us, the rest of the warriors with them.

"Malu," cried the Doctor, "is there anything we can do? What are these monstrous things—where are they going?"

"They go to the big caves in the mountains," said Malu. "They move fast—too fast for the Beautiful People."

"But they've got Mike," cried Jacky, "Malu—Nuna—they've got Mike! We *must* do something to rescue him! —please, *please!*"

"There is nothing we can do now," said Malu, "nothing. We must go back to consult The Center and the Wiser Ones. And if they permit it, The Voice will call together our people from the other cities among the hills, so that we can build an army to march against the Terrible Ones."

"Surely they will permit it," said Mac impatiently. "Mike is our friend—he is one of us. We must help him. They *must* permit it!"

"I think they will," said Malu slowly. "Not only because of Mike, but because it is bad that the Terrible Ones have been seen near our city. We have known for a long time that they have been assembling in the hill-caves to destroy us—now that they have begun to send out foraging parties they must be almost ready. We must strike before they strike—they are full of evil."

Mac and I looked at each other, then turned to stare across the plain. The receding enemy was almost out of sight, making for the hills far to the south of the glass city. All we could see, at that distance, even through binoculars, was a small red cloud. . . .

"Yes," said the Doctor, quiet again after his outburst of wild excitement. "We must go back—we must go back to prepare. We must get the *Albatross* to the city—we can't leave it unprotected in the plain here. And we must make arrangements to attack these hideous things somehow—we *must* help Mike. Oh my heavens, the poor boy to be with those unutterable creatures!—and the whole thing my fault, too!"

"Nonsense, Mac," I said. "It was one of those things—it wasn't anyone's fault."

"I brought him from earth," said the Doctor grimly.

"You *what!* Mac, you know perfectly well that he and the others stowed away! And by the same token, if anybody can do anything to help Mike in this mess, it is Mike himself!"

He smiled wrily.

"Perhaps," he said. "But we're the adults, Steve—we're the responsible ones. Come—we're wasting time. Let's go. . . ."

We turned around and made for the city, traveling in silence. Jacky's eyes were red from weeping when we reached the hills, and my own heart was heavy. I tried to keep cheerful, to put on an optimistic front for the sake of the others, but in my bones I felt that our hopes of ever seeing Mike again were very, very low indeed.

CHAPTER IX. ALARUMS AND EXCUR-SIONS

Part 1 by Stephen MacFarlane

A THEORY OF MARTIAN LIFE

Part 2 by Dr. McGillivray

FROM now on our story must begin to move rapidly towards its dramatic climax. So much happened, and happened in such rush and confusion that we cannot hope to give very much more than a general impression of it all—a description in any sort of detail would lengthen this book beyond all endurance.

But at this particular point there is a natural pause in the action—the inevitable calm before the storm. After the capture of Mike, and before his reappearance (you are bound to know, by the mere fact of his having contributed to this book, that he *did* reappear—though it was not without much danger and excitement, which you shall hear of anon)—during this time there was a period of preparation: more than a week, indeed, went by before there was any more positive excitement. And so this seems the natural chapter in which to insert Dr. McGillivray's interesting theory about the Martians and what they were—indeed, it seems to me that a knowledge of this theory is almost *essential* to a full understanding of all that follows. Before presenting the Doctor's paper, however, I want to write a few pages myself about what we did in the city towards preparing to attack the Terrible Ones—an attack which, as you will see, never developed, because of a sudden startling turn in events.

The first thing we did, then, after our return from the *Albatross* battle, was to seek an audience with The Center. Malu, Nuna, the Doctor and myself entered the huge central dome and moved respectfully to the mound where the controlling power of the Beautiful People lay. Malu began the interview by telling him of the battle and the capture of Mike (we did not "hear" this conversation, of course—all we knew of it was the slight sense of disturbance I have talked of as signifying, to us, an intercourse among Martians: but we knew from what The Center said to us later that this was what Malu had been describing to him).

When Malu had finished, there was a long pause while The Center looked at each of us in turn. The strange transparent flesh of his face was quivering, his small side tentacles writhed sensitively towards us. At length he said:

"It is bad that the Terrible Ones have come among us —it is bad that they have captured your friend, whom along with yourselves, you strangers from another world, we had welcomed to our city. Last night you, McGillivray, told me and the Wiser Ones something of your world: we, in turn, told you something of ours. Among other things we told you of our enemy, the Terrible Ones, who for so long have wished us evil. Now that you have seen the Terrible Ones for yourself, it must be clear to you why we fear them. Their presence near our city can mean one thing—they are assembling to destroy us. Before they can do that, it is our duty to destroy them; and therefore, The Voice will be instructed to assemble here, in the chief city of the Beautiful People in this part of our world, the warriors and picked men from all the other cities among and beyond the hills. And we shall march against the Terrible Ones in their deep hill caves and rout them out and end them—and rescue your comrade, too, if he has not been destroyed. Tell me now, McGillivray, is there anything that you want from us, so that you too can prepare for the attack?"

Mac took a step forward.

"Yes," he said. "I have told you of the vessel in which we came to you from our own world. It lies in the plain, as you know—it was because of the interest the Terrible Ones took in it that we went forth to fight them this morning. It must be brought here to the city to safety.

I cannot bring it without the help of your people. May I have that help?"

There was a slight pause, then The Center said:

"If it can fly—and you have said that it flew here through the skies—why may it not fly to the city from its resting place in the plain?"

"I cannot explain that to you," answered Mac, "until we have exchanged more thoughts with each other and know more of the sciences of our two worlds. But, speaking briefly, it is because the vessel will not fly for short distances—it is not built so. You must believe me when I say that I cannot move it here without the help of your people."

"You shall have that help," came the response, after another slight pause. "You shall instruct Malu in what you require, and he shall provide it if he possibly can. From time to time you will come back here to report to me on all that happens concerning your arrangements. For the moment, that is all."

Immediately, the wall of guards closed round the still, squat figure. We went out into the open air and set about our work at once.

The removal of the *Albatross* was our first consideration. The rocket was provided on the under side with huge steel skids, and it seemed to us reasonable to suppose that it could be dragged on them across the loose sand of the plain to the hills—even, if we could get enough labor, up through the forest (the track among the trees was wide enough) to the city itself. We explained the idea to Malu as well as we could, and tried to find out from him if there was anything in the nature of a rope on Mars. He led us outside the city to the hills, and there showed us the entrance to an enormous cave. When we went into it we found, to our astonishment, vast coils of a powerful fibrous cable, and—mystery of mysteries!— some huge wooden trolleys, low slung, mounted on rollers consisting of trimmed logs of the hardwood from the trees. These trolleys were shaped like gigantic T's, the long center bars being some seventy or eighty feet long, the cross bars perhaps fifty. To cut a long story short, I may say that we discovered eventually that these trolleys existed for the purpose of transporting the huge crystal domes from the place of their moulding among the hills to whichever spot the Beautiful People chose for a city. I shall say no more of this for the moment—it is one of the things the Doctor will be writing about in some detail later on in this chapter.

The removal of the *Albatross* took us two days. An immense group of the Beautiful People, led by Malu and Nuna, came across the plain with us, dragging one of the biggest of the trolleys to the hollow where the rocket lay (I might mention, in passing, for the sake of being thoroughly circumstantial in this account, that the ropes or cables, we discovered, were woven from the leaves of a coarse kind of grass that grew deep in the hills). We spent the first day in getting the *Albatross* out of the hollow. With the ropes noosed over it we found that it was possible for it to be dragged, on the skids, right across the floor of the hollow and up the slope of the ridge. The Beautiful People were magnificent workers—exceptionally strong for their size—and, after all, the rocket weighed little more than a third of what it had done on earth (a fact the Doctor had to take into reckoning later on when it came to setting off from Mars, incidentally—not nearly so much fuel was needed for the initial start-off from the surface). As the nose of the space-ship rose above the top of the ridge, we were able to manœuvre the trolley underneath it, and so, gradually, with the help of levers, and cables pulling in counter directions, we got the whole *Albatross* on to the great T-shaped carriage, ready for transportation across the plain.

We left it beside the hollow overnight, with a guard, and then, next morning—the fourth of our sojourn on Mars—we went out across the plain again with our great army of Martian laborers. Long cables were fixed to the cross-bar of the trolley, the Martians coiled their hand-tendrils round and round them, and so we set off. In spite of the great strength we were able to bring to bear because of our numbers, progress across the plain was slow: it was mid-afternoon before we reached the hills, and late evening before the *Albatross* finally came to rest on the little plateau overlooking the shining city of the Beautiful People. The scene during its transportation had been fantastic—hundreds of the small, energetic Martians pulling at the long, taut cables across the desert—it was like the paintings one has seen of the building of the ancient Egyptian pyramids: there too the transport had been by hand, and the great blocks of stone had been mounted on logs or rollers of wood.

The Doctor's next task was to build, beneath the *Alba-*

tross, on the plateau, a cradle, or launching ramp. He explained to me, privately, that he wanted this done lest by any chance the situation between the Beautiful People and the Terrible Ones should become so dangerous for us that we would have to escape suddenly. With the help of Malu's laborers he built up, from the tough trunks of the trees (great piles of these were lying, ready cut and trimmed, in the store cave in the hills), a sloping slipway on top of the great trolley—in other words, the launching ramp was built up gradually *underneath* the *Albatross*, so that we were not faced with the problem of having to move the heavy space-ship *on to* the structure. The job was a rough and ready one—the Martians had no very advanced ideas on engineering—but it was adequate. And the fact that the whole thing was mounted on rollers meant that every day the Doctor could make calculations apropos the relative positions of earth and Mars, and have the cradle constantly changed so that the nose of the *Albatross* always pointed in the right direction.

While all this was going on, there was great activity in the city. Groups of males were to be seen, armed with the long crystal swords, practicing leaping and slashing— a sort of militia drill, one might say. From time to time small regiments of warriors like Malu's contingent arrived from the hills, summoned presumably by The Voice. The Voice, as far as I understood it from the Doctor, who had had the whole thing explained to him during his first interview with The Center and the Wiser Ones, was the means by which communal or regional communication was carried out among the Beautiful People. How exactly it was done—whether The Voice was an actual being, like The Center—we never discovered: but somehow powerful telepathic messages could be sent almost any distance —they were so strong that they took precedence over any other thoughts going on in the minds of the particular group of the Beautiful People they were aimed at.

All the time, during the preparations for the attack, we humans went on living in the tent we had built just outside the dome assigned to us. The Doctor had ascertained that the leaves and spikes of the trees were quite edible —indeed, were extremely nourishing; and by dint of eking these out with an occasional tin of meat or fish from our store, we were able to feed ourselves quite satisfactorily. Just outside the trolley cave in the hills we found a small well of rather flat-tasting water, and so were well supplied on this count, too. In our leisure hours, sitting quietly in the evenings in our tent, we thought and talked about Mike, wondering where he was and what he was doing —if he were safe, or if the dreadful creatures who had captured him were maltreating him in some way—had killed him, perhaps, altogether. Yet somehow none of us could believe that Mike was dead—he was, as we remembered him, too vital and resourceful a character. We longed, above everything else, to set to work to rescue him, but however much the Doctor urged action at his meetings with The Center, he was told that the time was not ripe—all the regiments had not come in from the outlying cities.

So we waited. Gradually the city filled up. There was, in the atmosphere all round us, a sense of concentrated tension and anxiety—a mounting, subtle excitement. One night, just before we went into our tent, there was a sudden rumbling—as it seemed, in the earth beneath our feet. It lasted perhaps five minutes, and when we asked Malu what it was, he said:

"It is the omen of the mountain—the mountain tells us that it knows we are in danger, and will help us."

I looked at Mac in bewilderment.

"It's all right, Steve," he said with a smile. "It's a volcano, I think—a mild earthquake caused by a volcanic disturbance among the hills. This whole district is volcanic in the extreme—you can tell that by the shape of that big mountain overhanging the city—and there are great layers of lava all over the ground up by the store cave. Interesting, though, that they should think of it as an omen—it's the first sign we've encountered of superstitious belief among the Beautiful People. . . . I must remember to talk to The Center about it at our next meeting. . . ."

Yes, we waited—fretfully and impatiently. The only one among us who did not seem to feel the boredom of inactivity creeping over him was the Doctor. After he had seen the *Albatross* settled, he moved about among the Beautiful People, making enquiries, examining them, photographing them. He had innumerable conferences with The Center, he filled notebook after notebook with views and comments. In the interest of exploring a new field of scientific discovery, he grew more and more excited, and in the end he announced to me that he had formed a theory as to what the Martians were—"the only theory that fits all the facts, Steve—an astonishing theory, but a terrifyingly logical one—by heavens, but it will give them something to think about back on earth!—and it's so simple!—it's a wonder I didn't get it straight away —it would have explained so much! . . ."

Because it "explains so much" I am, as I have already said, setting out the Doctor's theory here, in the second part of this interval chapter before the final dramatic scenes of our too-brief visit to Mars. It is, as you will appreciate, extremely difficult for a man of science to set forth a complicated thesis in a very few pages, but in the interests of the lay reader I have, as before, asked the Doctor to keep his remarks as simple and concise as possible. This means that inevitably he will not be able to expand much, or set out many proofs in support of his opinions; but, as he himself said earlier, in reference to his paper on space flight, recourse can always be made to his numerous articles in the scientific journals by anyone wanting more detail.

Here, then, are the Doctor's notes. Anyone interested only in the actual story of our adventures on Mars can skip from here to the last few paragraphs of the chapter; if you do do this, however, I recommend that you come back later and read this paper of the Doctor's. My strong advice is that you will not skip at all: it seems to me absolutely essential for a reader to know what the Martians are at this stage of the story.

A THEORY OF MARTIAN LIFE
By Andrew McGillivray, F.R.S., Ph.D.

1. *General Introduction.* I wish it clearly understood at the outset that this paper is to be regarded as no more than a digest of the extensive writings on this subject I have already contributed to various journals since our return from Mars. Limitations of space demand that I be brief, almost to the point of baldness. I shall be unable to set forth in any detail the processes of observation and deduction that led me to form the theory I now propose to outline—I shall do no more than make a series of statements, which you are at liberty, in the absence of proof, to accept or reject as you see fit. Rest assured, however, that I do not make these statements in any mere spirit of caprice or whimsy: I am, after all, a scientific man, with a considerable reputation to lose.

The only thing I regret is that circumstances beyond our control rendered it imperative for us to leave Mars rather earlier than I personally had intended, as you will find as you proceed with the reading of this book. This means that my findings are not as fully documented as I might have wished. However, I propose, as soon as it may be arranged, to remedy this by returning to the haunts and homes of the Beautiful People (if, indeed, any such exist after the terrible disaster that befell those innocent and charming friends of ours!) so that I can indulge in more research.

146

With this brief preamble, I now set forth my views. I shall begin by discussing the planet itself—for, after all, as sociologists well know, environment is an immensely important factor in determining the shape of the evolution of any sort of life.

2. *The Planet.* I came to the conclusion, after certain geological researches, and many conversations with the Martian scientists (who are, incidentally, very well-informed on the universe in general and their own home world in particular), that Mars is a dying planet. The atmosphere is rare, and seems to be slowly—very slowly—dispersing altogether. Even more important than this, however, is the question of moisture. I did not have any chance to embark on personal exploration, but according to what I was told by the Martian scientists, and what we saw ourselves as we approached the planet and so could view it as a map, so to say, the main water courses run towards and round the poles. These seas, vast as they are at the moment, are drying up. The process, of course, will take many thousands of years, but nevertheless it is going on. The land masses, in consequence of this, are arid—vast deserts of dry sand and no more. The only vegetation is in or near the mountain ranges, and for the most part this consists of the vast cactus-like plants already described in these pages. The roots of the plants are prodigiously long, and are tuberous: by capillary action they bring moisture from deep down in the soil, and this moisture is stored in the great leathery leaves. Now and again, among the hills, there are slow-oozing wells—like the one we ourselves so fortunately discovered near the city—but

147

these are freakish and vestigial. The plants provide the only real irrigation system on the surface of Mars.

There are two seasons on Mars, a summer and a winter, quite clearly defined, each lasting some eight or nine months of our time. We were fortunate enough to land in the middle of summer in the district inhabited by the Beautiful People. Summer is a mild, pleasant season, very dry. Winter is much bitterer than our British winter. This fact has, as you will see, a profound sociological significance in the life of the Martians.

The mountain ranges—there are not many of them—are honeycombed with caves and tunnels, running far and tortuously into the soil. Most of the mountains are volcanic—actively so.

3. *The Inhabitants.* I come now to the point of setting forth the startling theory that has been referred to several times in this volume, by myself, by Mr. MacFarlane, and by Mr. Adam. I wish you, the reader, to bear in mind all that you have been told about the appearance and general characteristics of the Martians—particularly the Beautiful People. You will recall their *tendrils*—the thick, root-like ones that function as feet, the fibrous hand-tentacles, the short, sensitive, feeding-tubes. Recall the heated, steamy atmosphere of the domes—the "houses." Recall the one thing that baffled us at the beginning of our acquaintanceship with the Beautiful People—the fact that they seemed to have some form of telepathic communication with the cacti on the plain.

The answer to all these things is simple—bafflingly simple: *the Martians are plants themselves.*

Just as, on our planet, the animal form of life has evolved as the highest, so on Mars it was the plants that developed to the eventual exclusion of any other type of life. The Beautiful People are plants—flowering plants: even the Terrible Ones are plants—of a different genus, but still plants.

On the surface there would seem to be many objections to the theory. And, as I have said, I have not the space to adduce a series of proofs for my contention. It will suffice for me to say that I make this statement in all good faith, satisfied in my own mind that it is a true interpretation of the facts. Here are some general observations.

First, there is the question of the individuality and mobility of the Martians. Plants, as we know them, are static—they have their roots in the soil, and, for feeding purposes, the roots must remain there. Yet each Martian can move at will from place to place—and at considerable speed, as we have seen. The answer is that the Martians did begin as static plants many thousands, even millions of years ago—probably as a species allied to the cacti of the plain. In the long, long course of evolution they gradually, as they acquired perceptiveness, developed the power of moving—probably this was made necessary as the planet slowly dried up and they had to seek the moister districts. The movement at first was of an elementary kind—the development of certain root-tendrils as creepers, I fancy. I need hardly add that this creeping propensity is evident in a great many of our earth plants —without mentioning any of the numerous exotic varieties, I may cite the homely strawberry, the even more homely vegetable marrow (which has even been known to climb over garden walls!) and, among flowers, the iris and the convolvulus. In course of time the plants were able to move on their creepers without having to drop roots into the soil—they became detached. And from here it is an easy step to the Martians as we knew them—with vestigial creeper tendrils actually functioning as feet. The "hands" are also vestigial creeper tendrils. Of the small mouth tendrils—which still function as roots—I shall have occasion to speak separately in a few moments.

In this general connection of the evolution of the Martians, I may say that I had an occasion to see the whole process at work when Malu took me to see the young —the "children," so to say—of the Beautiful People. These were housed in caves in the hills near the city— huge deep caverns with a warm, humid atmosphere. The floors of the caves were, so to say, gigantic forcing beds— layers of decaying leaves from the trees, the "bodies" of dead cacti and so on (the atmospheric heat came partly from the decaying processes of this matter and partly from volcanic fires beneath the mountains). The seed of a new Martian is sown in one of these beds. It grows as a *plant*—the very new ones I saw were mere little greenish shoots, like almost any sprouting plant on earth. Gradually the roots through which these "children" are gaining moisture and nourishment from the soil, throw out creepers—the little Martians begin to move, literally to move, of their own volition, as they develop, to other beds nearer the entrance to the caves. Finally, one day, they become complete individuals—entirely separate: smaller editions of Malu, as it were. Then they come out of the caves and descend to the city to take up life as individual Beautiful People. This whole process of growth, of microcosmic evolution, takes some four to five years of our time, as far as I could reckon it.

It will not be inappropriate here to say a few words about the generative principle of the Martians. *This is the same as among plants on earth*—the same process of the transference of pollen from flower to flower takes place (without the intervention of insects, of course). The mossy tuft on the top of the trunk of a Martian is literally his "flower." We have seen that there are male and female Martians—in the female, the flower is larger and more beautiful. It will be possible now to visualize the whole process, to the point where the seed is inserted in the hot beds I have mentioned. Thus the great and marvelous universal principle of life is observed in operation in all its beauty and grandeur, on Mars as on earth—as, most probably, in each and every corner of the cosmos.

I shall deal briefly now with some other aspects of the Martians: their power of vision, for example. I assume that the "eyes" are certain cellular areas near the flower that began by developing a general sensitivity to light (our earth plants are sensitive to light in very broad terms —vide the sunflower). In the course of evolution these areas developed into recognizable eyes. As far as hearing is concerned, we found that the Martians sensed noise only if it were loud enough to provide a really concussive vibration of the atmosphere—they "felt" pistol or rifle shots, for example, or volcanic explosions—and they felt them with their whole bodies. But that was the only sense in which they could be said to hear—sound, to them, had not the significance it has for us.

Their feeding principle is simplicity itself. When their own roots began to function as creepers and then feet, they had to develop parasitic tendencies. Their own small feeding suckers, or roots, had to be attached to static plants so that they could draw nourishment from the soil *through them*. The principle can be observed on earth in the case of the mistletoe, for example, feeding on the oak. The feeding of the Martians, as we saw it in the cultivated cactus fields in the city, is, so to say, a temporary grafting process.

I close this part of my paper with a reference to the domes in which the Beautiful People lived. As time passed, and the planet on which they flourished began to die, so that the winters grew intenser, the Martians had to adjust themselves or perish. One miraculous day in their history they discovered a remarkable natural phenomenon among the hills—the event can only be compared in significance to the discovery of fire in the course of our own human history. The surface of Mars consists of sand, as we have seen. At certain points among the volcanic hills, the enormous heat of the subterranean fires instituted a fusion process of the silica in this loose crystalline soil. In this way a species of glass, hard and virtreous, was formed (the process of the manufacture of glass on earth will be familiar enough to most readers for them to perceive how this vast chemical process operated). In most cases the glass, as it cooled, hardened into lumps—sometimes, as it overflowed a rocky ridge, into long stalactites—icicles, so to say (these, sharpened by chipping, as were the old flint weapons of our cave-men, became the swords and spears of the Beautiful People). In certain places, however, an interesting thing happened. While the glass was still in a molten condition, the subterranean fires would burst through the surface in a minor volcanic eruption. The sudden release of gases blew the molten glass into gigantic bubbles. And when the gases had spent themselves, and the fires died, there, shining in the sun, were the huge crystal domes the Martians came to use as houses—literally as glass-houses—hot-houses.

In building a city, what they did was to choose a valley or hollow among the hills where some large domes already existed (in the case of the city we saw, the huge central dome had been blown on the spot). They then transported, by means of the large trolleys we have described, as many other smaller domes as they required from the various moulding grounds. Once a dome was in position, they dug, somewhere inside it, a deep shaft or well. This brought heat from the subterranean fires of Mars into the domes, and thus they were provided with the means of combating the altering weather conditions of the planet.

In winter, the Martians stayed almost all the time inside the domes, emerging only occasionally to feed (although they had cactus plants for most of the feeding necessary in the domes already), and to tend the "children" in the warm hill caves. In summer they moved

about quite freely in the open air, as we have seen, re-
treating into the domes at night and when they wanted
to rest.

4. *Concluding Remarks and Final Observations.* I am
aware of an immense amount of ground still to be covered. Having talked about the general physical character-
istics of the Martians, I ought to say something of their
social and political arrangements. Alas, there is no space
—and, I may also say, I did not have enough time among
the Martians to be able to acquaint myself thoroughly
with this immense subject. As soon as it may be arranged
I hope to return to Mars to investigate fully the many,
many aspects of a mode of life so vastly different from
our own.

For the moment it will suffice to say that the motivat-
ing force in a Martian community is The Center, a highly
developed and sensitive creature, seemingly ageless, capable of propagating himself (vide Mr. Adam's description
of him as having, on top of his stem, male and female
flowers together). He is, as it were, a kind of *Social Conscience*—I cannot be more specific than this; as I say, I
did not have time to go into this fascinating question
thoroughly. He communicates with his people by means
of The Voice—some sort of telepathic force I am unable
properly to define. He has, as advisers, a group of her-
maphroditic individuals similar to himself, who are known
as the Wiser Ones. These are, at the same time, the
scientists and the priesthood, so to say. They do all the
real thinking for the people—they control them and keep
them informed on all they need to know. The ordinary

Martian can think, but he cannot think really creatively. The Wiser Ones do this for him—as I have said, they are singularly well-informed about Mars itself and about the universe in general; that is why we were accepted quite simply among the Beautiful People as beings from another planet—it did not seem to them strange that there were such things, and that they had arrived among them. All they wanted to know was how the journey had been achieved, and something of the world from which we came. I endeavored to answer these questions to the best of my ability in the short space of time available to me during our conferences in the big central dome of the city.

As I say, I would wish to investigate further among all these things before writing more fully on the subject— the superstitions and folk-lore of the Martians, if any; their morals; their religion; their philosophy; their art forms—music (if such a thing is possible to them) and the visual arts. If I am spared I shall be returning soon to the scene of our recent adventures, and then I should be in a position to provide at least some information on these subjects, as far as my limited abilities will allow.

I conclude with a few remarks about the other life-species we saw on Mars—the creatures known as the Terrible Ones. They, too, were plants—they had solved the problem of combating the elements by living in the vast underground heated caves among the mountains. I did not have a chance to explore their methods of feeding at first hand, though I gathered from the Wiser Ones that they were parasitical, like those of the Beautiful People. My own view is that these creatures, the Terrible Ones, are descendants of a different species of plant altogether—probably something akin to our own insect-digesting plants: the Venus Fly Trap and the Upas Tree. This would account for the huge jaw-like petals which give them the appearance of having mouths. This would seem to indicate that there was, at one time, some sort of animal life on Mars. That it no longer exists I am convinced—the jaws are merely vestigial.

What really interested me about the Terrible Ones, however, was their wanton enmity to the Beautiful People. There was no obvious reason why they should wish to destroy them—they did not require them for food, for example. It was simply that they were full of an unreasoning malignance—that was as surely a function of their lives as an equally unreasoning benevolence was a function of the lives of the Beautiful People. It was an illustration of yet another great principle permeating the entire universe—a principle impossible to understand other than mystically: the principle of Good and Evil.

About this, one could write volumes. My own space, in this brief paper, has been used up—I have intruded on your patience too long. I leave you now to those who will continue the actual narrative part of our book—and I do so in the hope that these remarks, sketchy as they are, will in some degree illuminate what they have to say concerning the spectacular ending that fate gave our adventure on the Angry Planet.

A Tailpiece to Chapter 9 by Stephen MacFarlane. Our

period of anxious and impatient waiting came to an end very suddenly on the ninth evening after the capture of Mike.

We were sitting on the sand just outside our tent, watching a group of warriors drilling. The Doctor was writing up his notes, Jacky was mending a tear in one of Paul's shirts (we had brought needles and thread in the rocket with us), and Paul and I were commenting on the military display in front of us. Presently the Doctor looked up from his writing and called to me:

"I say, Steve, pass me over a drink, will you—I'm thirsty."

Lazily I reached over for the cannikin we used for storing water.

"Hullo," I said, "it's empty. Paul, you must have forgotten to go up to the well to fill it this afternoon."

"I'm afraid I did," said Paul. "I was just going to go, I remember, and then I saw Malu carrying some new swords over to the big dome, so I gave him a hand instead. I'll go up now—it won't take a moment."

"I'll come with you," I said. "I could do with a brief stretch-leg before turning in."

We set off through the city towards the store cave. When we reached it we set about filling the cannikin—a slow and complicated process this, since the well oozed so meagerly. We had almost finished, when suddenly, from quite close at hand, there was a hoarse shout:

"Paul—Uncle Steve!"

We looked up. Staggering towards us down the hill-slope from the forest was a tattered and grimy figure.

157

"My heavens!" I cried, "it's Mike! Paul, do you see—it's Mike!"

There was no doubt about it—Mike it was; a Mike all scratched and rather pale and haggard-looking, but still Mike. He staggered up to us, laughing and gasping a little hysterically, and shook us by the hand.

"Boy, am I glad to see you both!" he cried, over and over again. "How are the others—how's Jacky?—and the good old Doc?"

"They'll be a lot better for seeing you," said Paul with a grin. "What in the name of Pete have you been doing with yourself? We thought you'd have been killed off twenty times over by this time!"

"I as good as was," said Mike grimly. "Gosh, those things! Listen Uncle Steve, we've got to do something, and we've got to do it quickly."

"We *are* doing something," I said. "We're almost ready to set off to attack those monsters—there's only one more regiment of warriors to come in, and that's due tomorrow morning."

"To attack *them!*" exclaimed Mike. "Uncle Steve—they're going to attack us! They're all set for it—they'll be on the city in no time—hordes of them!"

His eyes were wide and he trembled excitedly. I could see he was suffering from strain—was even a little feverish.

"Listen, Mike," I said, "don't tell us any more just now. Wait till we get down to the city, among the others. Come on—we'll give you a hand. You can lean on me—I'll give you a cuddy-back, as old McIntosh calls it, if you like."

He laughed.

"We needn't go as far as that," he said, "but I wouldn't mind leaning on you—I must say I'm a bit done in. And if you've got anything solid to eat down there, I don't mind giving it the once-over—I'm famished."

Supporting him, we got him down to the city, where Jacky wept all over again—this time with relief at seeing him safe. Mike repeated to the Doctor and Malu what he had told me about the Terrible Ones being about to descend on the city, and those two went off immediately to report the danger to The Center. Mike, looking better already, after an immense meal that Jacky set out for him, started to tell us the story of his adventures.

He talked far into the night, while all about us the assembled warriors stood alert, waiting for the attack. The twin moons came up and circled the sky above our heads, and in their light we saw, on the plateau above the city, the shining, comfortable shape of the *Albatross*.

Mike's story was a strange and exciting one. You can read it in the next chapter as he wrote it himself after our return to earth.

CHAPTER X. CAPTURED! BY MICHAEL MALONE

(N.B. It says Michael up above and everybody knows I really prefer Mike, but somehow Michael looks better than Mike when it comes to putting it down on paper like that at the top of a bit of writing, you see. So I don't mind it for once.)

Well, now, here goes. I'm no writer—as a matter of fact I always get low marks for composition at school—and besides, it takes so long to write a great huge thing like a chapter in a book, and it hurts your hand after the first three or four pages.

I'll begin at the point where I jumped across the hollow to have a whack at old What's-his-name when he was getting ready to squash Nuna and break Malu in two. Well, the next thing I knew was being swung up into the air and then we were over the top of the ridge and tearing across the plain like mad. There's no doubt about it we moved at some speed all right—the Doc and Uncle Steve and Co. just didn't have a look-in, even notwithstanding (I asked Jacky about this word and she says it's all right to use it here)—notwithstanding the way they could jump about on Mars. I saw them left right behind as we went tearing over the sand, and then I lost sight of them altogether, it was so joggly being carried away up in the air. Besides, I was being held very tight. I felt my head swimming, and then in the end I lost consciousness altogether.

When I came to, we were among some hills and had slowed down our pace a bit. I was a bit groggy, I must say—I was sickish from the joggling and so on. We went along through some trees, and then we plunged into the mouth of a big cave. It was dark almost immediately, and very, very warm—there was quite a draught of hot wind coming along in our faces. We went down-hill for a longish time, and then suddenly it began to get quite light again and the tunnel opened out into a great big cavern—oh, huge. There was a sort of twilight in this cavern—I didn't know where the light was coming from at first, but I found out later that there were shafts run up from the roof into the open air, and some light filtered through them. But oh the heat in this place!—and even worse than the heat was the smell. This cavern was full of great monsters like the ones that had been in the hollow, and I'm sure the smell came from them—in fact, I know it did, for any time there were a lot of the things together there was always this smell. It was a sort of flat, horrid smell—it was like when you're walking through damp woods and you stumble on one of those big ugly yellow toadstool things and it breaks, and then there's a sudden nasty smell like this one I'm talking about.

Old What's-his-name put me down—well, chucked me down, rather—and there I was, in the middle of all those ugly great things—hundreds of them—all staring at me and sometimes prodding at me with their feelers. Uncle Steve has described them, so you can imagine I didn't feel too good. The one that had been carrying me—the one I call old What's-his-name—he pushed me along with his feelers through the crowd, and suddenly I was in front of a sort of mound, like the one The Center lay on back in the glass city, and on it there was a huge thing like a toadstool—one of the Terrible Ones, but much bigger than any of the ones I'd seen so far, and absolutely dead white and sort of clammy-looking. He was horrible—the inside of his jaws wasn't red, the way the jaws of the others were, but a pale kind of pink, like the underside of a mushroom.

Well, he looked at me for a long time, and then I realized that he was speaking to me. It was the same sort of thing as went on among the B.P.—you know, thinking it in your head kind of thing—but there was *something* different about it. I don't know what—it isn't at all easy to describe, but it was a sort of coldish thin voice you heard and there was a sense of badness in you all the time it was going on—it was almost as if the thought had a *smell*, if you know what I mean, like that awful decayed sort of smell I've been talking about.

So this big white fellow said to me:

"What thing are you? Why were you with the Enemy?"

(I found out later that these things always referred to the B.P. as the Enemy.)

So I said:

"I'm a human being, if you want to know—I don't suppose you'll have any idea what that means, but it's what I am all the same. And I come from the earth, which is millions and millions of miles away. I don't expect you'll understand that either, but I came from there with some friends of mine in the *Albatross*—and, if you want to know what the *Albatross* is, well that's out on the plain, and your friends were nosing about at it."

Well, he must have understood me a bit, because he said:

"What is the thing you call *Albatross*? What is its function? Our foraging party found it, as they have told me, when exploring on the plain."

"It's no use me trying to explain it all," I said, sort of bored (Jacky says "resigned" is a better word.) "You wouldn't really understand. The *Albatross* is a space-ship —for flying through space. And I can't tell you any more than that—maybe the Doctor could, but he isn't here."

There was a pause, and a sort of disturbance among all the things round about. And then the big one said, starting off on another tack:

"Did you come from the city of the Enemy?"

"Yes," I said, "if you want to know, I did."

And then a strange thing happened. They laughed—all those great hulking ugly things laughed! It was one of the most terrible things I've ever come across. You see, you somehow didn't imagine Martians laughing—laughing's something you *do*, it makes a *noise*, you know. And we hadn't had any experience of the B.P. laughing—it some-how didn't seem possible to laugh when you did all your talking and so on by thinking. But here they were—laughing. They didn't move—there wasn't any change in their faces. But in my head were those hundreds of thin, sort of snaky voices, all in a sort of nasty chuckling. And the big one said:

"In a little time the city will be no more. We are almost ready to attack it—it will be no more, and the Enemy will be broken. They cannot stand against us—in the past we have been too small in number. But now we have joined together—all of us who used to fight among ourselves. And we shall swallow them up!"

And they laughed again—on and on, for a long time. I felt disgusted with them, and frightened too, I don't mind saying. And besides, I was still a bit sickish from the journey, and then there was the heat, and the awful smell of them, too.

*   *   *   *   *   *

(These asterisks across a page mean passage of time—I learned that at school once. So I'm putting them in here, quite professional-like. In this case they also mean that the Author got a bit fed-up with writing for the minute —and he was hungry too, so he stopped and had some of Mrs. Duthie's pancakes. On we go then—and being professional again, I'm going to start this new part of the chapter in what my English master at school calls the "historic present.")

I am in a small cave just off the main cavern. It's quite darkish, and the heat is terrible. There's one of the great things that captured me lying across the entrance to the cave, so I can't get out. He just lies there like a great lump, but sometimes he turns round and stares at me with those eyes of his, sort of on stalks—he just stares.

Once or twice I try saying something to him—what do they think they're going to do with me, and all that— but he never answers. Twice some others of the things come for me and take me to the big toadstool chap, and he asks me some questions—who I am and where I come from—all that sort of thing all over again. The second time, after I'd done my best to explain about earth, and so on, I decide it's my turn to ask him some questions. I reckon that by now almost two days have passed—I was able to tell, anyway, that I'd spent one night in the place, by the way the cavern got dark, as I could see from my smelly little cave. I had had some sleep but they hadn't made any attempt to feed me—what was worse, they hadn't given me anything to drink, and what with the awful steamy heat in the cavern I needed some water pretty badly.

So I said to him—the big chap—that I was hungry and thirsty. At first he didn't seem to get the idea, but then after a time he did, and he and the others laughed again in that rotten way I mentioned before. And he says to me, how would I stop my hunger? Well, that was a poser —I just didn't know what to say to that. I thought of saying to them, what did they eat?—maybe I could eat the same; and then I remembered the B.P. and thought that if these chaps had the same sort of habits, that wouldn't be much good. And then suddenly I remembered the Doc saying something about the leaves on the big trees—how he was going to try them for food for us. And I thought, well—I might as well take a chance. If they're poisonous, that's just too bad—even dead I couldn't be much worse off than I am now, I thought, and if you're dead you aren't hungry—at least, I don't think you are—it doesn't seem likely, anyhow. So I said it was leaves I ate. They just couldn't get the idea. It seemed to be the word "eat" that was the difficulty—they could understand being hungry, and they could understand stopping hunger by taking something in, but actual *eating*, with your mouth (I pointed to my mouth and tried to explain with signs)—they couldn't understand that at all (I found out afterwards, by the way, that they did feed the same way as the B.P.—from plants, through little feelers, so that explains that). Anyhow, in the end I said, sort of desperately, that if they didn't let me have some leaves from the trees outside, I would die. And if they didn't let me have some water to drink I'd die.

And then they said—drink?—what was that?

Honestly! I felt like bashing their great silly faces in!

In the end I thought the idea of *well*, or *spring*, very hard in my head—I tried to get a picture of a well in my mind and project it (that's the word the Doc uses for this business of thinking things *to* people). And after a time it seemed to click. Old What's-his-name pushed me with his feelers down to the far end of the cavern and into a little sort of alcove. And there there was a small slow spring oozing out of the rock—only a very tiny trickle, but it was enough. I licked at it with my tongue while they all stood staring at me. It was horrible—quite warm, and it had a flat, sort of limey taste, but it was water, you know, and oh boy, did I need water!

Well, the next thing was the leaves. When I'd finished

drinking, old What's-his-name prodded me back to the
Big White Chief, and I found that while we'd been away
he'd sent one of his chaps up to the open air for some
leaves—there was a pile of them on the ground in front
of him. So I picked up one of them and had a nibble at
it—and I thought to myself, well, Mike, old chap, maybe
this is the end of you, and if it is, well, Three Cheers for
Old England and God Save the King. But it wasn't the
end of me after all. The leaves had a sweetish, mushy
sort of taste, like sleepy pears, in a way, and nothing happened—they didn't seem in the least bit poisonous. So I
tucked into them good, and then I felt a little better (still
a bit hungry, of course—fruit and leaves and things are all
very well, you know, but not a patch on a big plate of
bacon and eggs, for instance). All the time I was eating,
all those huge things just stood around and stared at me
again—it was uncanny. I suppose they were quite curious
and interested to see me busy at it in such a different
way from them, but you see they didn't *show* they were
curious or interested. They didn't have any kind of facial
expression. Paul has said somewhere that that was one of
the queerest and most uncomfortable things about the
folk on Mars—this business of no facial expression: and it
was even worse with these smelly toadstool fellows than
with the B.P., because, you see, the Terrible Ones had
more recognizable actual *faces* than the B.P. had, and so
you expected some sort of smile or sneer or surprise or
something on them.

Well, that was the eating and drinking problem solved,
at least—not very satisfactorily, but well enough to get

by. Old What's-his-name pushed me back to my little cave, and the guard flopped down with a soggy sort of thud in the entrance to it again. After this, every day they brought me a fresh bundle of leaves into the cave, and twice a day I was led down to the little well at the far end of the cavern so that I could get a drink.

And so the time passed—the "days and nights slipped into one another," as they say in books. I slept or dozed a lot—I expect it was the heat. Altogether I felt pretty rotten, I must say—I used to have bad dreams—and in the gloom of the cave I sometimes didn't even know if I was asleep or awake while I was having them. Oh, all sorts of things—too long to write about here. Besides, I doubt if I *could* write about them; nightmares are beastly things—it isn't so much what happens in them (sometimes you can't even remember that next day) it's the atmosphere of them, somehow. There was one I remember particularly—some sort of huge beast (it was a dragon, actually—it came from a picture in a school reader I once had) had caught me up in its jaws and was going to bite through me. It never got to the point in the dream where it *did* bite through me, but I could feel its hot breath all round my middle, and it was that that was the real nastiness of the dream. Ugh! I hate to think of it, even now.

Mind you, all the time the one thought that was uppermost in my mind was to work out some sort of plan of escape. Apart from just *wanting*, for my own sake, to get away from the Terrible Ones, there was another thing that was beginning to worry me quite a lot. Every now and again—on an average about once a day—I was led out to the mound in the cavern to be cross-questioned by the Big White Chief. He was always on at me about the earth, what it was like, and all that, but what he seemed to me to be really after was somehow to taunt me about the attack he and his followers were planning on the city of the B.P. They all seemed to get some sort of queer comic pleasure just from telling me about it, and boasting what they were going to do; they would laugh and laugh in that beastly mirthless way. As far as I could gather, as those conversations went on, the attack wasn't very far off. Foraging parties went out almost every day to spy out the land. It seemed to me that their plans were pretty nearly complete—the Big White Chief actually told me once that they were waiting for some "special fighters" to come in from some far-off caves, and then they'd set off through the hills to have their whack at Malu and Co. Well, as I saw it, if only I could escape and warn the B.P. of just how dangerous the situation was, it would be a good thing all round. I was worried about the Doc and Uncle Steve and Paul and Jacky, to say nothing of the B.P. themselves. There were hundreds and hundreds of these great nasty things in the cavern, and the Big White Chief had told me there were thousands more, in other caves close at hand.

The problem was *how to escape?* All the time I was in my own little cave, the guard was slumped across the entrance, and when I was in the cavern it was always crammed to overflowing with the monsters. To make any sort of dash for it would be right out of the question—I wouldn't get more than a few yards. Even if, by a miracle,

I got into the passage-way leading down to the cavern, they would overtake me in no time—I remembered from the time of my capture just how fast they could move.

Well, I brooded and brooded. And it wasn't for a very long time that I began to see a faint glimmering chance of how it might be done. When I did think of it I could have kicked myself, because in a way it was so simple— I should have thought of it right away. It's funny, you get used to things you know—I'd got so used to sitting still in that little cave, and walking about with ordinary steps in the cavern, that I had almost forgotten I was on Mars and could *jump*. Yes, *jump*—and jump pretty high at that! Thinking along those lines I suddenly remembered something else; and I decided that next time I went out to have a chat with the Big White Chief I would keep my eyes skinned—just to see if it was all going to be possible.

But it wasn't for another couple of days that I was called out to an interview—and I've got a feeling it wasn't meant to be an interview! Before this, though, something rather curious happened.

One morning, the guard at my cave mouth shuffled aside and three of the Terrible Ones came in. They were different from any of the creatures I'd seen so far; they were much smaller, to begin with, and they were lighter in color—not yellow-and-red in spots the way old What's-his-name was, but almost white, like the B.W. Chief. For a long time these three chaps just stood staring at me, then they moved quite close and began to feel all over me with their tentacles. It was a horrible sensation—little

170

soft, gentle pattings and strokings. I edged away from them as far as I could, but they followed me right over to the wall.

Quite suddenly they stopped and stood back and stared at me again for a time. Then one of them picked up a tree leaf from the pile that had been brought to me that morning and held it out to me. He said:

"Eat!"

I thought it was a bit odd—especially the word "eat," since that was the word I'd had difficulty over with the Terrible Ones at the beginning. But I was feeling pretty peckish anyway, so I ate the leaf as they had asked me. And while I was chewing it, blest if these things didn't come close up to me, and one of them put out two of his feelers and pried my mouth open! Then they all three peered down my throat for a time. I didn't like it in the least little bit, but what could I do? When I raised my arms to take the feelers away from my mouth, one of the other ones wrapped his tentacles round me and there I was—pinioned—and they were as strong as horses, those things.

Well, after a time they went away, but they came in the evening and went through the whole performance again. This time, after I had eaten a leaf, one of them took one up himself and put it between the two great pink jaws he had. Slowly—very very slowly—the jaws closed. He stayed with them closed for a time, and then, just as slowly, he opened them. The leaf fell out on to the ground, a little bit crushed but otherwise none the worse (which isn't surprising, considering these things had no teeth inside their jaws only the little soft knobs—sort of taste-buds, as Uncle Steve has called them a couple of chapters back).

Next morning these three chaps appeared again, and then, the following morning early, they turned up with old What's-his-name, who immediately set about prodding me out of the cave. I was being taken to the Big White Chief.

As we went across the cavern I realized that old What's-his-name was speaking to me.

"There is one more day," he said, "one more day, and then the city of the Enemy will be no more. This night we shall set out, and to-morrow we shall fall upon them and destroy them." Then he paused, and added: "And you shall not be there to see."

I didn't like the sound of this at all. What did he mean? Was it just that I was to be left in the cave, and so wouldn't actually *see* the attack, or was there something else behind it all? I must say I felt a bit uneasy. There was another thing too. All about us as we moved among the monsters, there was a sort of *tension* in the air—it was as if they were kind of expectant about something. And they were bad—they were just plain *bad*; there was just a sort of nastiness in the whole atmosphere.

We reached the mound where the Big White Chief lay. And now the sense of danger and badness was so great that I could hardly bear it. Old What's-his-name, instead of stopping me about ten feet away from the mound, as he usually did during an interview, started pushing me very slowly towards it. And it seemed to me that the huge pink jaws of the big fellow were open just a little bit wider than usual.

It was all a bit too much for me. And I decided not to postpone my plan of escape any longer but to have a whack at it there and then.

I had remembered, you see, when I recollected I could jump, that just above the Big White Chief's mound there was one of the long light-shafts that led down into the cavern from the open air. It was about twenty feet from the ground, in the sloping roof. I had noticed, during my interviews, that the walls of it were rocky and irregular—there was just a chance that, with my reduced Martian weight, I'd be able to find enough foot-hold to scramble through it to the surface.

I was barely a yard from the jaws when a sudden panic came over me and gave me just that necessary spurt to act. With all my energy I jumped. The height was too great for me to cover in one leap—I had realized that from the beginning. But you see, there was the Big White Chief, on his mound, and he was a good ten feet high.

The first jump landed right on top of his shell. Just for a moment I felt my feet sinking into his soft pulpy flesh, and then I jumped again—straight for the shaft entrance. It was now or never. I scrambled and scratched desperately for knobs and crannies to cling to, jumping and pushing all the time sort of hysterically. A little way up, the shaft bent over in a slope, and that helped a lot. Somehow—I don't know how—I managed it. How long the shaft was, or what time it took to get through it, I just haven't the faintest idea. All I do know is that after a nightmare of heaving and struggling I was out in the open air, on a hillside, panting and gasping and feeling dizzy in the head.

I was free—absolutely alone under the blue sky. And so far there was no sign of any sort of pursuit.

Well, that's really the bulk of the story—there isn't very much more to it than that.

When I got through the top of the shaft I made immediately downhill a little for the shelter of some trees. Just as I reached them I saw a bunch of the Terrible Ones come pouring over the hillside from the cave entrance below. They snuffled and peered round the shaft for a while, then they all stopped and stared in a direction a little to my right. That gave me the idea that that was probably the direction of the B.P.'s city—the monsters would have assumed that I was making for it, and so were looking for me along that line. It was the way I certainly took as soon as they dispersed from the shaft and went down the hillside again.

Traveling through the mountains wasn't at all easy. The forests were very thick in places, with strange plants in them—clumps of tall grasses, for instance, very fibrous and twiney, with an unpleasant sticky surface. There were sudden ravines that you came on most unexpectedly—some of these I was able to jump, others were just too wide, and so I had to scramble down them, cross the floor, and then scramble up the other side. Once or twice I came across foraging parties of Terrible Ones in the early part of the journey—on one occasion I had to jump

was free—absolutely alone under the blue sky

up and hide among the thick foliage of a tree while a group of them passed right underneath. And, of course, to crown all, I was very anxious and worried as I traveled —as I saw it, it was up to me to get word to the B.P. as soon as possible that they were going to be attacked. Would I make the city in time?—was I, after all, going in the right direction?

Well, the day went on, and then, in the evening, when I was beginning to think that it was all no good, and that I must be miles and miles away from Doctor Mac and the rest, I suddenly rounded a shoulder and saw, shining beneath me, the glass city! And barely a quarter of a mile away, drawing water at a little well, were Uncle Steve and Paul! I let out a yell and rushed down the hillside towards them.

And there we are—this is where I came in, so to speak. This is the point that Uncle Steve had reached in his chapter about what happened while I was in the hands of the Terrible Ones. I'll leave it to him again to describe what happened the day after my escape, when the great ugly brutes attacked us—for they carried out their plan, as old What's-his-name had told it to me; they marched from their caves during the night, and in the morning—

But I'll leave it to Uncle Steve, as I said. For my part, I'm glad this long chapter of mine is over. It's taken such a bally long time to write—and yet I suppose you'll only take ten minutes or so to read it. Who'd be an author—it's such a fag!

Well, I hope I haven't bored you too much. It was a bit of a nightmare, eh?—all those toadstooly chaps. Still, in a way, I'm glad it happened to me—it's given me some-thing to tell the fellows at school. Of course, I was lucky enough to escape and all that—well, if I hadn't, I wouldn't have had anything to tell—or rather, I'd have had a lot to tell, only I wouldn't have been here to tell it. So that's that.

Well, cheerio, and all the best

Yours sincerely,

Mike Malone.

(*A Note on Chapter 10 by Dr. McGillivray.* When I read the manuscript of the chapter you have just pe-rused, I asked my young friend's permission to add a brief postscript to it. I had two reason for doing so: first, to congratulate him on having written a most patient and edifying account of his adventure, and second, to offer, in all humility, an explanation for a part of that adven-ture that seems to me to need clarifying.

I refer to the strange episode of the examining of young Malone by the three lighter-colored monsters.

My interpretation of the whole incident is this:— You will recall, from my paper on the nature of the Martians, that I am of the opinion that the creatures called the Terrible Ones evolved from plants similar in type to the insect-eating plants of our own planet. I deduced from this, if you remember, that at one time there had been animal—or at least insect—life on Mars. As it died out, the Terrible Ones adapted themselves accordingly, keep-ing their big jaw petals as lingering relics of the days when they had subsisted on flesh (that they were just a little more than vestigial ornaments we have seen from Michael's description of how they could open and close them).

Now it seems to me that it is just conceivable that lingering somewhere in the deep race-memories of the Terrible Ones, there was a dim, imperfect recollection of their carnivorous days. *The sight of Michael eating probably brought this memory to the surface* (there is a certain superficial resemblance between mouth eating and the digestive processes of fly-catching plants). The three examiners I take to have been scientists or priests—the equivalent among the Terrible Ones of the Beautiful People's Wiser Ones sect. They were examining Michael to see what he was made of—if he was *flesh!*

And I firmly believe that in the end they decided he was of that substance their ancestors had consumed. I believe they decided to try to consume him themselves! —or have him consumed by their leader. What superstitious and mystic intentions of sacrifice for victory might have lain behind the whole idea I do not know—as I have said, one of the things I most want to explore is this whole spiritual aspect of the inhabitants of Mars.

At any rate, if I am right—and I am certain that I am —it seems clear that if Michael had not contrived to escape when he did, he would have been submitted to the truly ghastly fate of being *digested alive* in the jaws of the great creature on the mound!

Let us be thankful that through his youthful energy and resourcefulness he managed to get away in time.— A.McG.)

CHAPTER XI. ATTACK, BY STEPHEN MacFARLANE

The Assyrian came down like a wolf on the fold,
And his cohorts were gleaming in purple and gold . . .

IT FALLS to me now to describe the last tragic day of our sojourn on Mars. It is impossible not to feel sad in writing of it, as the spectacle rises in my mind's eye of the crude destruction of so many hundreds of the Beautiful People. We had not been with them for long —little more than a week of our earth time; but somehow, in that space, they had endeared themselves to us. Their way of thinking, their whole approach to life—these things were utterly charming and simple. Paul has used the word "innocent" in describing them, and that indeed does seem the only suitable adjective. Their unthinking benevolence (which one *felt* all the time one was with them), their acceptance of things—these were character-istics that made a profound impression on us. Why they called themselves "the Beautiful People" it is impossible to say—it was things like their definition of such an epi-thet as "beautiful" that we were on the brink of exploring when we had to leave. But that they were beautiful—in our sense of the word—there was no doubt at all in our minds.

And so many of them were annihilated!—utterly swamped and destroyed! It has often seemed to me strange that we arrived on Mars so shortly before the desolating of the Shining City. If we had set out, for in-stance, when we first intended to, how different our im-pressions would have been, with no Beautiful People to welcome us—perhaps only a few remnants of the Terri-ble Ones, lurking in the hill caverns or among the ruins of the glass domes. No doubt eventually we would have found our way to one of the other cities, deeper among the mountains. But that would have taken a long time—the shape of our visit would have been totally different.

For a brief spell we lived in a pastoral and delightful way; and then, in one day—one morning—we saw that sister world of ours live up to its name of the Angry Planet.

We stayed awake right through the night of Mike's re-appearance. We sat quietly in the tent after he had fin-ished the account of his adventures, the Doctor and I smoking endless pipefuls of tobacco, the boys feeding a low smouldering fire we had built for comfort in the sand. Jacky, I remember, sang softly to herself. There was something unutterably strange in the thin plaintive sound of her voice going drifting among the quiet domes and losing itself in the hills. She sang many songs—the old ones we have all been accustomed to since our cradles—songs that are so familiar that we forget that someone once ·actually wrote them: songs like *Barbara Allen*, *John Peel*, *Swanee River*, and *Sally in our Alley*. But over and over again she came back to a song that was her own favorite—the haunting old nursery song:—

> *The Owl and the Pussycat went to sea*
> *In a beautiful pea-green boat.*
> *They took some honey,*
> *And plenty of money*
> *Wrapped up in a five-pound note* . . .

All the time, in the light from the two moons, we were aware of the still shapes of Malu's warriors all round us. The females and the ordinary males had gone into the domes as usual to spend the night, but the warriors were awake and on guard, standing in silent groups with their long crystal swords outstretched in readiness. The atmosphere was full of a sense of expectancy—the tension was unbearable. Malu, close to us, seemed to lean forward slightly as he strove to catch a message from the planto ringed all round the city that the danger was close.

The night passed. The moons grew dim and sank out of sight behind the hills. Now the landscape was flooded with the gray twilight of the Martian dawn, and presently the sun rose over the horizon—exactly as we had seen it on the first morning of all. The sky grew clear and blue, the warmth came back to our slightly chilled limbs.

Mike yawned and rose to stretch himself.

"Well, it seems as if I was mistaken," he said. "Either that or they've come to the conclusion that I'll have warned everybody and so called off the attack. I vote we have something to eat, and then—"

He got no further. At that moment there came a sudden stiffening in the ranks of the warriors. And we, in our nervousness—our feeling for the community in which, for better or worse, we found ourselves—heard in our heads, swamping every other thought in them, the insistent message:

"Danger—danger—danger! The path by the store cave—danger!"

It was our only experience of The Voice. It came to us, I am sure, because in that moment we were exceptionally highly strung and sensitive. And because too, in a mystic sense, we had that day become part of the Beautiful People.

Malu and the warriors turned and stared towards the hills at the point where Mike had appeared the evening before, and we too—all five of us—strained our eyes in that direction. For a long time nothing happened, and then, suddenly, there was a movement among the trees. And a moment later there came into view a huge white shape, sickly in the sunlight—a monstrous swaying toadstool, it seemed.

"The Big White Chief!" yelled Mike. "It's the Big

A huge white shape—a monstrous swaying toadstool

White Chief himself! And there's old What's-his-name beside him—I can tell him by that whack that Nuna gave him in the side!"

Surely enough, beside the white monster, there now appeared one of the Terrible Ones, his bright yellow-and-red coloring standing out vividly against the sandstone brown of the hillside and the somber green of the trees. And presently another appeared, and another, and another, until there was a closely-packed wall of them, staring down at us.

"My heavens!" muttered Mac at my side, "what beasts they seem—what unutterable beasts! It's impossible to believe they're plants, Steve—cabbages!"

"What are we going to do, Mac?" I asked. "There are hundreds of them—we hardly seem to have a chance."

"We can't do anything but defend ourselves," he said grimly.

"With what?" I demanded. "Our guns don't seem any good."

"No, our guns are no good—bullets are too small for these things—they're plants, and haven't any one set of vital organs. The only way to destroy them is to shear away the tissue, the way we saw Malu and Nuna do. We'll have to arm ourselves with swords, Steve."

"But the children, Mac?—what are we going to do with them? We can't expose them to this danger."

"We'll have to make for the rocket," he said. "Jacky and the two boys can go up into that, and you and I will stay at the foot of the ladder, to help Malu as much as we can. We'll have to rely on the warriors—and the only

184

thing is, they're not quite so helpless as they look beside these monstrous things, as we saw out on the plain."

He spoke grimly, and his jaw was set. I was finding hidden depths in this quiet and reticent character!

We moved towards Malu, and I explained briefly to the children as we went what our plans were. We had just reached the central group of warriors, and were choosing swords from the great pile that lay near them, when suddenly there was a wave of movement all along the enemy line high up on the hillside. At an incredible speed the front rank of the monsters rushed down towards the city, their tendrils flailing. And behind them came other ranks, dividing in two streams on either side of the white leader. There was no end to them—they came up in masses through the trees and poured towards us like a liquid, their pulpy bodies glistening in the sunlight. It was a terrible, a freezing sight.

Malu's warriors stood motionless. And then, at the moment when the enemy reached the foot of the slope, the front line of them—arranged in a huge arc before the outermost domes of the city—rushed forward and joined battle with the advancing monsters. From where we stood, we saw nothing but a melée of flashing swords, of writhing tendrils, of green and yellow-and-red bodies. And as in the fight for the *Albatross*, our heads were full of a high, terrifying screaming.

This first phase of the battle lasted no more than a few seconds. The impact of the onrushing monsters was too great for Malu's slender fighters. They went down beneath the wave, struggling valiantly but uselessly. The enemy advanced into the city—and still, behind the front ranks, more and more of them poured down the hillside, the white swaying leader moving more slowly in their midst, a ponderous and implacable Juggernaut.

On the level ground within the city the monsters slowed their pace. Moreover, they had now encountered Malu's second line of defence—a thick wall of warriors packed tightly among the outer domes. The very density of this line withstood the shock of the attack, powerful as it was. For a moment the antagonists seemed inter-locked—it was body to body—then suddenly the various statuesque groups of the fighters disintegrated, and the scene became violent and contorted, with warriors leap-ing high into the air to deliver the death blows to the monsters, and the monsters in their turn striving to get their tentacles round the slender trunks of the Beautiful People.

All the time, females and non-fighting males were pouring out from the domes on all sides of us. They ran, in panic-stricken herds, behind the central group of war-riors. We, in our position, were in danger of being jostled and crushed by them as they fled.

"Make for the *Albatross*," yelled Mac in my ear. "It's all we can do!"

I nodded, and seized Jacky by the hand. Then, signaling the boys to follow, I started to struggle through the seeth-ing mass of the Martians.

The *Albatross* lay on the little plateau above the city—fortunately for us, in the opposite direction from the point where the Terrible Ones had appeared. We heaved and fought our way past the domes, occasionally jumping high over the heads of the Beautiful People when we encountered a knot of them too compact in their panic to be broken through. Eventually we reached a point where the crowd was thinner, and then, in great strides, we leapt forward and started to mount the slope towards the plateau.

When we were halfway up we saw a sight that made our hearts sink. The rear ranks of the Terrible Ones, on the opposite slope, were no longer pouring into the city. They were splitting into two huge arcs and were moving round the city. In a few moments we would be caught, as it were, in the jaws of a gigantic pair of pincers!

Malu saw the danger. It would be fatal if the enemy once got into a position to attack on all sides—to pour into the city as if into a saucer. With part of the central group of warriors, the leader of the Beautiful People started to rush to the point where we ourselves were standing.

"Get to the rocket," yelled Mac. "Steve—for the Lord's sake!—we must get to the rocket!"

We jumped forward, and in a moment we were on the plateau, with the whole confused and terrifying scene spread out below us. Mac sprang to the swinging ladder and swarmed to the top of it to unlock the door. Then he descended again, and at the moment when Malu's group and the first of the Terrible Ones to circle the city joined in furious conflict on the slope just beneath us, Jacky hastened up the ladder and disappeared into the safety of the *Albatross*.

"You next, Paul," I shouted.

"Not me," yelled Paul, "I want to stay. I haven't had a whack at these brutes yet!"

"Don't be a fool," cried Mac. "This isn't any time for heroics, boy—get into the *Albatross* when you're told."

Before any of us could say another word there came a sudden pause in all the seething activity in the city below. We looked down—and there, in the very center of the scene of conflict, we saw a sight the memory of which haunts me terribly to this day.

Out of the vast dome in the middle of the city had crawled the creature we knew as The Center. He stood with his flaming crown a stab of vivid color even among the violent colorings of that scene, and he held in his front tendrils a huge crystal sword—a twelve-foot streak of light, like a great electric spark, as it glistened in the sun. Facing him—towering above him—was the white and evil shape of the leader of the Terrible Ones.

The two great creatures faced each other. And on all sides the battle seemed to die, as deadly enemies paused in their struggles to watch the symbolic duel being fought. The fleeing crowds stopped dead and turned to stare.

For a moment there was no movement. Then suddenly, with an energy that seemed out of all proportion to his bulk and flabbiness, The Center jumped. High into the air he soared, and as he fell he brought down his sword with terrible force straight across the face of the great thing facing him. One of the huge pink jaws fell clean away, and into our thoughts, even from that distance, there came a scream, icy and penetrating, of rage and pain and sheer malevolence.

The Center, with surprising agility, slewed sideways to avoid the tentacles that now shot out from the side of the white monster to encircle him. He shuffled and gathered his feet-tendrils for another leap, but before he could execute it successfully, the white monster, with another beastly scream, slithered in a pulpy heap from before him.

Too late The Center tried to adjust his aim. He lost his balance and stumbled. And in that moment the white monster acted. It was his turn to leap. He hurled his enormous bulk into the air, soaring like a monstrous and obscene bird. And he fell with a terrible squelching thud, horrible to our physical ears in all the silence of the scene, full on top of The Center.

And then, before any more movement could be made —before any of the contestants could resume the struggle—there came another sound—another actual sound, *in* our ears. Muffled and terrible in that supreme moment, it was a vast rumbling explosion. And all around us the ground shook and trembled, so that we had, in a sudden panic, to cling to each other for support.

Simultaneously the sky, which up to now had been blue and pellucid above the scene, grew suddenly dark, and a great gust or wave of heat seemed to rush in the air all round us. And from the top of the biggest of the mountains which overhung the city there poured a sudden fountain of flame.

"My heavens!" yelled Mac, white and staggered in the

unexpected gloom, "it's an eruption! Lord help us, Steve —the volcano!—the volcano!"

I did not answer. My eyes were fixed in horror and fascination on the slope down which the Terrible Ones had rushed to attack us. Pouring down it now, swift and menacing, was a seething, glowing tide of lava. And all round us were falling vast smoking boulders—some of them thudding among the bodies of the close-packed Martians, some crashing through the great glass domes, leaving huge jagged holes in the curved surfaces, through which poured volumes of smoke—presumably from the deep-dug heating shafts that led now, not to gentle subterranean draughts of warm air, but to a raging inferno of molten rock.

I saw once, in Italy, a live volcano: but there was nothing in its slow eruption that could compare with the violent agony of this great hot sore in the body of the Angry Planet.

How to describe the terrible scene that followed? The lava, sizzling and bubbling as if it were alive, poured into the doomed city. As it lapped round the bases of the great domes, one by one they seemed to melt and sink into nothingness—immense shining bubbles, red in the reflected light, subsiding and vanishing in the tide. Contorted figures, caught in the molten fingers of this implacable beast—Beautiful People and Terrible Ones alike—poised for a moment in a brief agony, and then sank into the stream. The dreadful liquid crept and oozed over the entire floor of the city—the saucer of the valley became a seething cauldron—a vast and terrible witch's brew.

Enormous tremors shook the earth

All this—this first part of the eruption—lasted only a few seconds. When it was over, the second phase began. Enormous tremors shook the earth, and the boulders began to fall more densely. Beneath us, on the slope leading up to the plateau, were some hundreds of Martians who had escaped from the lava—warriors and Terrible Ones, females and non-fighting males of the Beautiful People; and they all were struggling, as well as the heaving earth would permit them, to clamber up to where we ourselves stood by the *Albatross*. The awful thing was, that even now the lust to destroy in the Terrible Ones had not been satiated; even while struggling to save themselves they rushed among the Beautiful People, wrapping their tentacles round their slender trunks and either breaking them in two or casting them down into the hissing lava at the foot of the slope. Even as I looked at the scene, I saw one small hapless creature being swung high into the air and then cast far out in an arc to fall into the tide—and I recognized her, with a stab, as Dilli, the little female whom we had met when first entering the city.

"Steve," yelled Mac, "we'll have to get into the rocket. We'll be hit by one of those boulders—we'll be destroyed. Get the boys up the ladder—and hurry!"

I nodded. Paul and Mike had heard him too, and in an instant Paul had started to mount. Mike followed, and, when he was half-way up, I jumped on to the lower rungs myself.

As I climbed, a boulder shot past me—I felt the terrible heat of it in my face, and heard the thud as it buried itself in the sand of the plateau. I looked down. Mac was just mounting the ladder—the boulder had missed him by inches.

"Mac," I yelled, "are you all right?"

"Yes," came his answer. "Hurry, Steve—hurry or we're lost!"

I jumped the last few feet and staggered into the cabin. Jacky, white-faced, was crouching on one of the beds. Paul and Mike stood by the doorway, staring at the ghastly scene below. The whole rocket was vibrating beneath the trembling of the ground—it was a miracle that the improvised cradle on which it rested had not collapsed long before.

The Doctor swung himself over the lip of the doorway. His face was pale, his hair flew wild, his eyes stared in horror.

"Oh my heavens," he groaned, "this is dreadful—dreadful! These poor creatures! . . ."

"What are we going to do, Mac," I cried, shouting at the top of my voice to be heard above the crash of the explosions. "Are we going to go back to earth?"

"There's nothing else we can do," he moaned. "I hadn't wanted to, yet. There's so much to do here—so much work! But we're lost if we don't go—there isn't any other way to escape. We must pray that this ghastly shaking hasn't changed the direction of the cradle."

"Mac," I yelled, "couldn't we expend only a little fuel —enough to take us into the stratosphere—and then stop and land somewhere else where there isn't any danger?"

"You know as well as I do that that isn't possible, Steve —the *Albatross* can't be controlled for short flights—once we start we're into space, and once we're in space we've got to travel on till we reach earth—if we ever do reach earth. It's the one——"

He got no further. At this moment there was an explosion louder than any we had heard so far—it was as if the entire mountain were blowing up. As I staggered under the terrific impact I saw that the whole scene was suffused with a red and angry glare—an immense spout of flame shot skywards from the big mountain-top.

And immediately after the crash there was a yell from Mike.

"Nuna—Nuna," he cried, "I'm coming—hold on!"

And he was over the side of the rocket again, scrambling down the ladder. In horror the Doctor and I rushed to the doorway and stared out. Below us, hideous in the glare, a dreadful scene of conflict was in progress. Nuna and one or two others of the warriors had reached the plateau, and swarming on to it after them were some half-dozen of the Terrible Ones. One of these—a gigantic creature with an entire jaw and an eye missing—had twined his tentacles round Nuna's trunk, and in the implacable way we knew, was bending him back and back to break him.

It was this the quixotic Mike had seen—he was rushing to try to save Nuna, as once before he had rushed to try to save Nuna.

"Mike—Mike—come back!" I yelled. "It's useless, Mike —it's useless!"

194

But he paid no attention—I doubt if he even heard me. With his sword flashing red he was across the plateau in one great leap. Once—twice—the red blade flashed—the first time it severed the long cruel tentacles, leaving Nuna free to stagger backwards and collapse in a heap a few yards from the foot of the ladder; the second time it bit deep into the shell of the monster. With the haft sticking out of him like the haft of Excalibur from the anvil, he reeled to the edge of the plateau and went tumbling into the lake of lava.

Mike in an instant leapt back, and, catching Nuna round the trunk, dragged him desperately to the foot of the ladder. Somehow he got the slender limp form over his shoulder and started to climb—we, above, staring down at him in a helpless amazement. The whole episode had taken only a few seconds—we had hardly had time to recover from the first shock of Mike's sudden action.

Mike, struggling and breathless, was half-way up the ladder. And now—final horror—we saw that under the pressure of the last huge spurt of flame, the lava was being forced into the air and was falling over the entire scene as a fine deadly rain—the volcano had become a veritable fountain of lava. And simultaneously with our noticing this, we saw that one of the Terrible Ones had reached the foot of the ladder and was gathering himself for a spring—a spring that would carry him full on to Mike's back and drag him down to a certain death.

It was Jacky that woke us from our fascinated immobility.

"Pull," she screamed, "pull the ladder! Uncle Steve—save him, save him!"

The Doctor and I jerked into action. We seized the end of the ladder and, exerting a desperate strength, pulled it towards us. Thank heaven for the weaker force of gravity on Mars! Our first great heave brought Mike and Nuna to the door. Paul and Mac grasped them and dragged them into the cabin. I stood back a little, the ladder still in my hand—and suddenly it ripped out of my grasp, searing and tearing the flesh of my palms. The monster below had jumped!

We looked over the side. The hideous thing had not been dislodged by the jerk of the falling ladder. He clung with his tentacles and feet-tendrils to the rungs—and slowly, inexorably, he was mounting the swaying steel cables towards us.

"Mac," I cried, "is there no way to release the ladder—does it unfasten?"

"No," he shouted. "It's fixed securely—I never thought there'd be any need for it to be detachable. Oh my heavens!—my heavens!"

"Shut the doors," I yelled. "We can start even if the monster is hanging on."

"The weight will pull us out of direction. Steve, we've got to get rid of it—we've got to!"

Wildly he pulled the revolver from his belt. He fired six shots into the face of the thing below—six clean round holes appeared in the pulpy flesh. But still the creature mounted.

Then suddenly the end came. We saw something hurtle through the air in a great leap and land on the back of the monster. It was Malu!—Malu, who had seen our danger and has rushed to save us!

For a moment the two Martians clung together on the swaying ladder. But Malu's sword had bitten deeply into the Terrible One as he leapt, and the great flabby creature loosened his grip. As they fell to the plateau a message flashed into our heads—with one superlative effort, Malu—our first friend on that strange and terrible world —projected a last thought to us in that high dramatic moment. Not one of us but heard it clearly, cutting through every other thought in our crowded brains:

"Farewell, strangers—good journey! Remember Malu the Warrior—Malu the Tall, Prince of the Beautiful People. . . ."

We slammed the doors. Mike, his face and clothes burned by some of the rain of lava that had fallen on him, had collapsed in a heap on the floor of the cabin beside the still form of Nuna—but he was smiling happily, unconscious as he was. Jacky was sobbing—Paul stood dazed beside her.

Mac staggered to the control panel. He raised his hand to touch the lever that would launch us into space again. I looked through one of the lower port-holes for a last glimpse at the terrible scene. I saw, in that moment, that Malu had disentangled himself from the creature of the ladder—he stood swaying on the plateau, his sword swinging. Even as I stared I saw two more of the monsters advancing towards him menacingly. He was indomitable as he faced them. . . .

The Doctor pressed the lever. There was a rushing, explosive sound, drowning all else. The scene faded from my view—I knew no more than I know now of the fate of Malu. Did he escape?—or was he swamped by the monsters that rushed to overwhelm him?

For a moment a red mist swirled about the portholes. Then I felt myself losing consciousness. As I sank into oblivion my last thought was that even in these few seconds we were hundreds and hundreds of miles away from the Angry Planet. . . .

CHAPTER XII. THE RETURN TO EARTH, BY VARIOUS HANDS

1. *Stephen MacFarlane.* And so it is finished—"like an old wife's story," as the playwright has it. In that high moment, when Malu flung himself on the great yellow-and-red monster, our adventure on Mars came to an end. What follows is anti-climax—and must necessarily be so. In books, in plays, there is the contrived "curtain"—the dramatic peak of action, when all the threads are gathered together in one great explosive point: in life there is no great point—the curtain never falls. We have our moment of drama; we stand poised—but not for ever. Life goes on: we turn a corner, and eat, and sleep, and tie our shoe-laces, and it is all the same as before.

That is the way it was with us. There was the jerk as the *Albatross* leapt from the heaving surface of Mars, and there was, immediately, for each one of us in the cabin, the sense of unbearable pressure I have described already in talking of our flight from earth. We lost consciousness—and one of us, alas, never recovered from the sudden shock of that desperate start. Numa, weakened already under his wounds, and in any case much frailer than we were, and probably with organs of respiration less easily adaptable than ours, lay immovable on the floor of the cabin long after we had recovered and were shakily adjusting ourselves for another long spell of inter-stellar flight. Mike—none the worse for his collapse, and the slight burns he had received from the raining lava—moved shakily over to the limp shape of his friend, whom he had risked so much to save, and called him by name. There was no reply—no thought came into our heads from the still figure. Mike put out a hand to touch the little Martian, and immediately he went floating up into the air and stayed against the steel wall, bouncing gently against it. And we saw, unequivocally, that he was dead —he had died quite simply in the moment of acceleration. Mike's effort had been in vain. That Nuna had been alive when Mike brought him into the rocket there was no doubt—we had seen him moving before his collapse. But he was no longer alive—he bounced and floated in the cabin with the same air of forlorn helplessness I have seen in a goldfish that has died in its bowl; his tendrils waving limply, his glaucous eyes all dulled. There was nothing we could do. With sorrow in our hearts we laid him gently in a corner of the cabin, strapping him to the floor.

This done, we stayed quiet for a while, our heads full of unspeakable thoughts. We did not look at one another, but sat or stood with our heads bowed, preoccupied with the visions we were seeing. We were, I believe, a little crazed in the first hour—the impact of the horror of that last scene on Mars had been too great—intolerable in its effect on us and our reactions. It was already a thousand miles and more behind us, but still I seemed to see it, stark and brilliant before my eyes—the spouting lava, the great shining bubbles collapsing and melting,

the writhing limbs and agonized bodies of the Martians
. . . above all, the terrible spectacle of the leaders of the
two great species confronting each other: the squat, flaming figure of The Center, the monstrous, jelly-like bulk
of the chief of the Terrible Ones, white and evil, pulsing
with sheer malevolence.

It passed—in time it passed. We returned to normal.
We were once more, in outer space, weightless—but this
time there was no joy, no sense of adventure. It gave us
no pleasure to be able to bounce round the cabin, to un-
dergo the curious experience of eating from the "tooth-
paste tubes." In short, the long return journey had a
weariness in it—some sort of sense of defeat and frustra-
tion. There was so much we had wanted to do—so much
we had not done. All about us was infinite space—a great
velvet expanse, immeasurable, full of terror and mystery.
The sun shone golden against the deep, deep azure, the
stars were silver buttons, unwinking, in a vast and ever-
subtly-changing kaleidoscope. But somehow this—yes,
this unutterable glory—was old, old news to us. We
longed only for the journey to end—although all the time
we were haunted by the thought that perhaps it never
would end; perhaps, in all the trembling of the plateau
on which the *Albatross* had rested, the launching ramp
had changed position sufficiently to throw us out of
course—perhaps we would travel forever, never resting
till the end of things—going nowhere. . . .

But in time this terror passed too. We saw, behind us,
the great shining disc of Mars, which, at the outset, had
loomed hugely over our whole range of vision—we saw it

dwindle till it seemed no more than a red, glowing tennis-ball—till eventually it was a mere speck, a star among the rest. And we saw the other star—the one we knew for earth—grow proportionately larger, shining in silver like the moon, a burnished sphere against the dark velvet of space. It grew till we saw its shining poles—till we vaguely perceived the outlines of the continents. And we knew that we were safe.

Almost four weeks elapsed between our departure from Mars and the moment when Mac told us that we were well within the gravity-belt of earth, and that he would soon be switching on the nose *tuyères* to retard our flight, and pushing out the *Albatross's* wings so that our landing would be smooth. Quite where we were going to land he could not say. In the limited time at his disposal for manœuvring he would be able to make roughly for Britain, but he was not altogether sure if there would be enough fuel to get us there (if you remember, we did not switch off the engines when we ought to have done on the journey out, because of all the turmoil and excitement of discovering the children, and we had therefore used up some of our precious fuel; and although this had been counteracted, to an extent, by the fact that we had not needed a great deal of fuel in starting from Mars, because of the smaller gravity-pull, the two things had not quite cancelled each other out—we were just a little on the debit side).

We entered the swirling white mist I described when writing of our outward flight. The Doctor and Jacky adjusted their masks—Paul, Mike and myself strapped our-

We landed the Albatross in Northern France

selves to the beds and waited, as stoically as we could, for our brief bout of unconsciousness. The Doctor reached up to touch the control levers. Beneath us, dim through the swirling mists, I saw indistinct patches of green and blue, and, for a moment before my senses left me, a corner of earth—a map, as it were—that seemed like the northern coast of Africa, with Gibraltar jutting out as a stubby finger from Spain towards it.

And then all went blank once more. When I regained consciousness it was to the realization of a great sliding bump and tremor. Then all was still—for a moment, painfully still. We had arrived—we were back home—on earth. We were among our friends again. . . .

* * * * * *

As the world knows, we landed in the *Albatross* in Northern France, at a small village not far from Cherbourg, called Azay. The story of our sudden appearance out of the blue, and our landing in a field in which three old peasants were working, is altogether too well known to require any repetition here. The old people were simple-minded, honest souls who accepted the *Albatross* quite willingly as some new type of airplane, but were utterly astonished to see five people—two adults and three children—descend from it and go rushing round their familiar field like lunatics. Jacky was laughing a little hysterically, I remember, and crying too, at the same time, and as for me, well, I confess it unashamedly—I got down on my hands and knees and actually kissed the good brown earth, digging my nails into it deeply and letting

204

the loose damp soil, so different from the remorselessly dry soil of Mars, go running through my fingers! All this is old news now—there have been endless accounts of it all in the papers, with photographs of the *Albatross* resting in the field with ourselves beside it, with the old peasants—the Picaults—beside it, with the Mayor of Azay himself beside it; photographs of the Picaults giving us wine and milk after our arrival (specially posed the following day, actually, but counterfeiting quite successfully, as far as the Press and its readers were concerned, the real occasion); photographs of the *Albatross* being dragged by huge tractors from the little farm, being swung by great derricks at Cherbourg docks on to the ship that brought it, and us, to England.

All this has been told and retold a hundred times, and would be stale in the re-representation here. We have, all five of us, broadcast our accounts of the arrival, our impressions on landing on earth again after so many weeks in space. We have addressed meetings up and down the country, we have been banqueted and fêted—particularly the children; we have been filmed and televised—we have even made gramophone records for a well-known company, complete with sound effects supposed to represent (not very successfully, I fear) the swishing, explosive sound made by the motors of the *Albatross.* At the beginning of this book—this holiday task of ours—I said we would write only of the things not properly covered so far in the various accounts of our adventures that have appeared: that, in short, we would set down our honest impressions of the journey as it affected us individually. That task is done—our holiday after the great (and embarrassing) welcome we were given is at an end. We have not, in any sense, in the preceding pages, attempted to *explain* anything: we have simply, each in his own manner and style, set down our thoughts, our accounts of our reactions and experiences. Inevitably this book is sketchy. How can it be otherwise, being so short? Inevitably, too, it is merely the prologue, the harbinger of others. As I have already said, the Doctor is engaged in the compilation of a volume of some bulk that will set out, for the more scientific reader, an account of his innumerable valuable findings, both in space and on Mars—that will, among other things, provide an amplification of the theory on the nature of the Martians he has sketched for us in these pages. I may add that I myself am beginning work immediately on a much fuller version of the entire adventure than these present jottings present you with, and I have a feeling that Jacqueline, who is, by general consent, the most literary-minded of the children (although, by a paradox, she has contributed least to this volume), will be embarking on a long personal essay on the whole episode. She, during the memorable days of waiting on Mars, had much intercourse with the two little females we were introduced to by Malu—Lalla and Dilli. I know that she has much of interest to communicate on the subject of the domestic life of the Beautiful People. She also was able to collect, and note down, one or two of the haunting folk tales of these strange creatures—it is possible that she may be in

206

a position soon to publish these separately in book form, either as a collection or individually.

Until these more comprehensive volumes are ready (and, because of the vastness of the subject, it may be some time before they are), this present book must stand as an earnest of our intentions—a scenario, as it were—a synopsis of the full, detailed story. As such, it comes now to its natural end, imperfect though it may be in many aspects (for instance, I have not dwelt at length on the return journey, partly because it was in the main uneventful, and hardly different in general shape from the somewhat fully described outward flight, and partly because, for us, the adventure may be said to have ended when Malu freed us from the incubus of the thing on the ladder at the height of the volcanic eruption). It will remain only, in the final pages of this last chapter, to set out one or two documents concerning our arrival—letters, diary entries, and so on—that will, perhaps, strike a more intimate and personal note than the flaming headlines that announced to a startled world only a few weeks ago:

MAN'S FIRST FLIGHT TO MARS
SCOTS PROFESSOR AND WELL-KNOWN WRITER ACCOMPLISH SPACE-SHIP JOURNEY IN TWO MONTHS
THREE CHILD STOWAWAYS ON BOARD

These notes and jottings now follow. With them we say good-bye to you, our patient readers, and to this book, which, it must be admitted, has given us much joy in the compilation: for, in the evenings, here in my quiet little Pitlochry house—the house I feared I would never see again when first the Doctor and I set out—we have regaled each other by reading aloud the various chapters as they were written, living over again, as we did so, our adventures on that infinitely strange and different world millions and millions of miles away.

2. *Miscellanea.*

A cablegram from Jacqueline Adam to her mother, Mrs. Margaret Adam, at Upton Minster Nursing Home, Dorset:

CHERBOURG

ALL WELL STOP PAUL AND I HAVE BEEN TO MARS STOP ALL OUR LOVE JACKY STOP.

A cablegram from Mrs. Margaret Adam to Miss Jacqueline Adam, Cherbourg:

UPTON MINSTER

DELIGHTED TO HEAR FROM YOU MY DARLINGS STOP DADDY AND I THRILLED BY NEWS JUST SEEN IN PAPERS STOP ALL OUR LOVE STOP HURRY HOME MUMMY STOP.

A cablegram from Mrs. Marian Malone to Michael Malone:

LONDON

AUNT MARGARET HAS JUST PHONED ME NEWS YOU NAUGHTY BOY COME HOME SOON STOP HAD TO RETURN FROM ARGENTINE WHEN YOU WENT MISSING STOP DADDY WILL BE FURIOUS STOP LOVE TO UNCLE STEVE STOP LOVE MOTHER STOP.

The Return to Earth

A cablegram from Dr. Marius B. Kalkenbrenner to Dr. Andrew McGillivray:

CHICAGO

CONGRATULATIONS ON REMARKABLE ACHIEVEMENT STOP COMING OVER TO CONSULT STOP.

A letter to her mother written by Jacqueline Adam from her aunt's home in London:

My darling Mummy,—It's very probable that we shall be seeing you almost as soon as this letter reaches you, if not before it altogether. But that doesn't matter in the least little bit—this letter is not meant to be full of news, for there is far too much of that to be written down—it will all have to wait till we meet. It is just that I am so terribly excited at the thought of seeing you again that I must just say *something* to you straight away.

As you can see from the address we are at last at Aunt Marian's house in London. We had to come straight here from Cherbourg because there is so much to do—they want us to broadcast, for one thing, and then there are all the newspaper people to be seen. But Paul and I have said that we are not having any more of it. The broadcast is tomorrow night (be sure to listen), and immediately it is over we are going to come down to see you—Daddy is going to bring us, I heard him discussing it all with Uncle Steve when he arrived from Dorset this morning. People are arranging all sorts of things for us—one of the newspapers is fixing a lecture tour all over the country, and although Paul and I said we were no good at lecturing (imagine us trying!), they said we ought to go all the same, that people would want to *see* us at least, even though Uncle Steve and Doctor Mac did all the actual talking. So we may have to leave again soon to go on this tour (the newspaper is making all arrangements for us to get off school for it, so that's not a bad thing), but anyway we are going to have at least a few days with you—we insist on that absolutely.

Oh Mummy, I can't tell you how lovely it is to be back again! It has been a wonderful adventure in many ways, but it was very terrible too, and I'm very glad it's over. Sometimes, you know, I can hardly believe that it happened at all—and yet at other times it all comes back in a sort of wave and I know I shall never, never forget it, not as long as I live. Some of the people of Mars were lovely—I wish you could have seen them, or that we could have brought them back with us. You would have been very fond of Lalla and Dilli, my own two special friends. Oh, but it isn't any use talking like this—it *is* all over, and it *did* all happen. And we're back again, among all our own people. It's so wonderful to see everything just exactly as it was before we set off—somehow, when we were looking at the earth from Mars, and it was only a star, it wasn't possible to think that places like London existed at all—even that Britain existed. But here it all is, not one little bit different—and oh, how good it is to be able to sleep on a real bed again, and to be our own weight, and to eat proper food, not leaves and tinned stuff and the vitamin pastes out of Doctor Mac's toothpaste tubes!

Aunt Marian has been very kind. She pretended to be a bit angry with Mike at first—she said he *must* have been the ringleader, and that if he had behaved himself it probably wouldn't have happened to us at all. But that was all just hot air. She was really terribly glad and relieved that nothing serious had happened to us, after all the worry of thinking we had been lost up in the hills at Pitlochry. Doctor Mac took all the blame—he said it was all his fault, that he should have looked over the *Albatross* thoroughly before setting off and that he probably would have found us then. Aunt Marian thinks he is "sweet," so really she has completely forgiven Mike and the rest of us, it's only that she likes to make a bit of a fuss. Besides, I believe that secretly, in her heart, she was glad to get back from South America—she didn't *really* fit in there. And then of course there's all the excitement of the newspaper men and the B.B.C. people coming all round the house to interview us—she's having the time of her life, if truth be told—you know the way she is.

Well, I really must stop, Mummy darling—it's time to go to bed. I can't wait till I see you. I hope you're very much better—Daddy says you are, that you are almost on your feet again, and that probably seeing us will complete the cure altogether. Oh Mummy, I hope so! All our love till we meet—   Your loving daughter,   Jacky.

Script of an interview in the B.B.C. radio magazine series, *In Britain To-night*.

> (*Fade up signature tune and opening sound sequence. Fade slowly out as announcer speaks.*)

Announcer: In Britain To-night! One of the most thrilling stories of recent times has been told in the Press these past few days—the story of the flight to Mars by Dr. McGillivray, of Aberdeen University, Mr. Stephen MacFarlane, the writer, and three children, Paul and Jacqueline Adam and Michael Malone. The three children are in the studio with me now, making a brief microphone appearance. Dr. McGillivray and Mr. MacFarlane will be giving talks in our programs in the course of the next few days, describing life on Mars and what it was like to travel through space. Meantime, we thought you would be interested to hear the voices of the children. Here they are.

Interviewer: Well now, children, perhaps you had better introduce yourselves to begin with.

Jacqueline Adam: My name is Jacqueline Adam and I come from Dorset.

Paul Adam: And I am Jacqueline's brother. My name is Paul.

Michael Malone: I'm Mike Malone, of London. I'm the youngest of the party.

Interviewer: It's true, isn't it, that you stowed away on board Dr. McGillivray's space-ship?

Jacqueline Adam: Oh yes. It was Mike's idea, really. You see, we didn't really know that Dr. Gillivray was going to Mars.

Michael Malone: My idea was just to have a look round

the rocket, you see, and then before we knew where we were, we had started off and were thousands of miles into space.

Interviewer: And what was it like to travel in space?

Paul Adam: It's very difficult to say. Actually, that's one of the things that Mr. MacFarlane will be able to talk about much better when he comes to the microphone. As far as we were concerned, I think the really exciting thing was not having any weight.

Interviewer: Not having any weight? Why, what do you mean?

Paul Adams: I can't explain it technically, but the thing is that once you get outside the gravity pull of earth, you are as light as a feather. We had to wear magnetic boots in the rocket to keep ourselves from floating about in the cabin.

Interviewer: That must have been grand fun.

Michael Malone: Oh it was! We very often took the boots off for a lark, and went for little flights in the air.

Interviewer: It sounds like something out of a fairy tale. And then, when you landed on Mars itself, what was it like?

Jacqueline Adam: Quite different from anything we could ever have imagined.

Interviewer: You met some of the Martians, of course?

Jacqueline Adam: Oh yes. We were with them in one of their cities for more than a week.

Interviewer: What were they like?

Jacqueline Adam: We got on very well with them. Of course, it isn't possible to describe them in the few moments we have on the air, but we have told the newspapers all about it— you can read about it in them. And Dr. McGillivray will be describing them when he talks over the air. But they were really very charming and kind to us.

Interviewer: Well, Miss Adam, it has been most interesting to chat with you, and I'm sure our listeners will have enjoyed hearing your voices. What are your plans now that you are back on earth?

Jacqueline Adam: We have to go on a lecture tour with Dr. McGillivray, but before that Paul and I are going down to Dorset to spend a few days with our mother.

Interviewer: I'm sure your mother will be very proud of you. And after the lecture tour, what then?

Paul Adam: I think we shall all deserve a holiday then.

Interviewer: Hear, hear! Does that go for you too, Michael?

Michael Malone: Well—to tell you the truth, if it's a matter of a holiday, I wouldn't mind going back to Mars to have one there!

(They all laugh. Fade into music.)

A letter from Mrs. Duthie, of Pitlochry, to Mr. Stephen MacFarlane:

The Return to Earth

Dear Mr. MacFarlane,—I was very relieved to get your letter for which I thank you and to know that you and the children will be coming up to the cottage for a wee rest after all your stravaging up and down the country lecturing to this one and that one. I read all about your trip in the papers and heard you talking on the wireless it really was very like your voice it was exactly as if you was in the room with me and it was a real relief to hear you although I thought you sounded a bit run-down, I expect you have not been looking after yourself and it will be the food in those hotels too, it's never what it should be, and them charging the earth for it—I tell you it is exactly what my Mother used to say when she was alive, these hotel people are like the Gordon Highlanders, they know how to charge. Well, Mr. MacFarlane, you are to take care of yourself and you are to look after the children, poor little things, imagine them going all that way to those outlandish parts and not having anyone proper to take care of them—and then eating leaves off trees too, it can't be good for anyone all that sort of thing. But it is a real relief to know that you are all safe and sound, I can tell you we were real worried about you, losh me it caused a terrible stir in the town when you went missing, and McIntosh had search parties out in the hills for days. The Doctor's labritary assistants, if that is how you spell it, they said when we heard an explosion and then they saw that the rocket thing had disappeared, well they said that you had all gone to the moon or that something had exploded, but we thought they were daft and went on looking all the same, but of course we did not

215

find anything and it has been a mystery ever since and in all the papers too till suddenly we heard that you had turned up again. Well, I shall close now, and tell the children I shall be having a lot of special bakings for them when they get here, and that will do them good and fatten them up a bit, there is not any doubt that growing youngsters need their food, that is what my Mother always used to say.

Well, let me know what train you will be arriving on and I shall see that McIntosh meets you at the station with the trap, Yours Truly,

Elspeth Duthie.

An entry in Paul Adam's notebook:

. . . Well, it's all over. In a few days we will be finished with this tour, and then it will be Pitlochry and a long rest. By Jove, a bit different from the last time we went to Pitlochry! Uncle Steve has suggested that while we're there we might all club together and write a book —a chapter each, sort of thing, while it's all fresh in our minds. Not a bad idea, I must say—I won't mind having a whack at an occasional chapter. Funny, I never thought of myself as anything of a writer, but take this notebook, for example. I started it as something to do on the journey out to Mars, and now I've got used to the idea of jotting things down from time to time—a sort of diary, like that chap Pepys they tell us about at school. Well, this is the last entry I'm going to make in it—we're almost back to normal now. It will certainly be something to

216

show my grand-children (that is, of course, if I ever have any!).

Well, that's the lot. I don't quite know how I ought to finish—maybe I should take a solemn oath that everything contained herein is truth. I think it would be best just to say cheerio, so that's what I'll do. This is the end of Paul Adam, his Notebook.

A letter from Michael Malone to Mr. McIntosh, game-keeper, Pitlochry:

Dear Mr. McIntosh,—Mrs. Duthie will likely have told you that we are coming to Pitlochry in a few days. I'm looking forward to seeing you again, but before I do there is something I have got on my mind, and that is why I am writing this letter. I've had a guilty conscience about it all the time we have been away on Mars, and I kept on wishing I could get in touch with you somehow. Do you remember that just before we left I borrowed one of your salmon gaffs—an extra big one it was. As a matter of fact, this whole adventure would probably never have happened if you hadn't lent me the gaff. You see, we used it for climbing over the wall of the stockade at Dr. McGillivray's laboratory. And then, when the rocket started off, there it was, still hanging on the wall, with the rope fixed on to it. So I never had a chance to return it to you. I hope you didn't need it too much and that you weren't angry with me.

I thought I would just drop you this little note of apology before we met, so that maybe you wouldn't feel

217

too sore about the gaff and not speak to me or something when we come to Pitlochry.

Hope your rheumatism is not troubling you too much these days. Yours sincerely,

MIKE MALONE.

A letter from Hamish McIntosh, gamekeeper, Pitlochry, to Michael Malone:

dear Mr. Mike,—i am not good at the writing so this is to say do not wory about the gaff she was an old one indeed when you come you can keep her as a suvener i am glad you are well i found the gaff on the wall. when i was looking for you. i shall meet you with the punny at the station i am not ofended about the gaff i remain your obedient servant

HAMISH MCINTOSH.

3. *Concluding Remarks by Stephen MacFarlane.* There is one more thing to be said, and this I have kept deliberately to the last, because it seems to me to be the one episode that gathers up symbolically in itself the whole evanescence, as it were, of our story. As I sit at my desk here writing, chewing over the cud of our crowded reminiscences, this above all is the image that haunts me— even more potently than the image of that first fight between the Beautiful People and the Terrible Ones, I think, or the flaming mind's-eye picture of the last great battle in the Shining City.

In all our interviews with the Press, with distinguished scientists, with representatives of the various film companies and the B.B.C., the one thing we were invariably asked was, had we brought with us any relics of Martian life. You who know by this time the extraordinary and sudden circumstances under which we left the Angry Planet, will realize that there was no time for us to collect anything—even a sample of soil—to bring back with us. Had we been left to our own devices we would have laden the *Albatross* with relics, as you can well imagine—it is inconceivable that a scientist of Dr. McGillivray's acumen would have omitted to do this. He was, indeed, engaged, as I well know, in compiling a huge stock of samples during the period while we were waiting for the Beautiful People to assemble themselves to attack the Terrible Ones. In our tent by the dome there were neatly labeled articles of every sort—leaves from the trees, small specimens of the cactus plants, pieces of the glass-like substance the domes were made of, even some seeds of the Beautiful People, and two very young sprouts from the great nursery-cave among the hills—in short, every conceivable thing likely to be of interest to enquiring minds on earth.

But our tent, and all its contents—these were overwhelmed by the lava. Nothing at all was conveyed to the *Albatross*—all we had stored in it, against a possible sudden emergency, was some water from the well.

Of our cameras, all but two were destroyed by the lava —and when we reached earth, and set about having the films in these two developed (they were of the 36-exposure-per-spool type, so allowing for the few exposures not made, there would have been some 60 odd photographs of the Martian scene available—a goodly number)—it was only to find, to our chagrin, that some deleterious quality in the rare atmosphere of Mars had rendered the sensitized emulsion quite useless—the films were absolutely blank. Dr. McGillivray has written extensively and learnedly on this unfortunate aspect of our adventure in the *Photographic Journal*—I mention the circumstance here only by way of explaining why the obvious course of illustrating these writings with actual authentic photographs has not been taken. Another thing that was destroyed by the lava, incidentally, was our portable recording equipment: but since, as we have said so often, there was no actual *sound* on Mars—no speech—this apparatus had been entirely useless to us: we did not make one single disc with it.

No, we had nothing to show—absolutely nothing.

But—and here's the rub—I can hear you say: But Nuna—Nuna was in the rocket with them—Nuna was a specimen better than any other—an actual Martian.

Nuna, alas, never reached earth with us. Nuna exists no more—the body of Nuna has been disintegrated beyond all hope of reconstruction—Nuna has vanished, has become an imperceptible dust, scattered in the enormous wastes of space. It is the dissolution of Nuna—the last glowing moment—that haunts me in the way I have already mentioned. Let me, quite simply and detachedly, describe how it happened—let me set it out here as the last scene of our book. . . .

Nuna never recovered from the shock of our start-off from Mars—this I have already given an account of: how

he was strapped to the floor of the cabin when we found
that he had died. On the third day of the journey, we
began to notice a sickly heaviness in the atmosphere of
the *Albatross*. It intensified. On the fifth day it was so
potent as to fill us with nausea—and we could no longer
disguise from ourselves the fact that we all had realized
secretly in our hearts but had been unwilling to mention
to each other: the body of the little Martian was decom-
posing—was, in doing so, poisoning our precious air. . . .

There was only one thing we could possibly do. Mac
and I, with heavy hearts, steeling ourselves to the effort,
unstrapped the frail limp body and took it to the inner
door of the cabin. Jacky and Paul turned away, so as not
to have to watch us, but Mike kept his face in our direction, though I could see that he was biting his lip, poor
boy. We opened the inner door and laid Nuna against
the outer one. Mac had contrived, at the outset, a device
for getting rid of things from the rocket while it was
traveling in space, though there had been no occasion to
use it on the journey out. It consisted of a heavy spring
between the inner and outer walls of the *Albatross* that
could be attached to the object to be ejected and controlled in its release from the inside of the cabin once
the inner door had been closed and the outer door opened
(the movement of the outer door could also be controlled
from inside the cabin while the ship was traveling).

We set the spring in position, and closed the inner
door. Mac touched the lever that opened the outer door,
and then immediately set the spring in operation that

would push Nuna into space. Then, with a sigh, he closed the outer door again. Nuna was no longer with us.

And now I come to the amazing part. When I looked through the port-holes beside the doors, it was to see, to my utter horror, that Nuna was still there—traveling alongside us a few yards away from the *Albatross!*

"Mac," I gasped, "what has happened? Look—look! He's there—outside!"

Mac spoke quite softly and simply.

"Steve," he said, "it can't be otherwise. Don't you realize, man, that there isn't any gravity in space—there is nothing to pull Nuna away from us. By the process of inertia, any object we put out from the rocket while we travel will travel with us—on and on—Nuna will go with us like that, where the spring pushed him, until——"

"Until what, Mac?" I asked, as he hesitated.

"Until we reach the atmosphere belt of the earth. And then," he lowered his voice still further, "well, Steve, although he seems quite motionless, Nuna is traveling as fast as we are, and you know what an incredible speed that is. You know what a shooting star is—a particle of matter traveling in space that suddenly comes within the gravity pull of earth, and then, as it shoots towards it, is made white-hot for a moment by the friction of the atmosphere, then is burned up. Nuna is not protected as the outer shell of the rocket is. When we reach the outer atmosphere——"

"My heavens, Mac," I said, "you mean . . . ? Oh, it's horrible, it's horrible!"

The Return to Earth

But however we felt, the thing had to be faced. If we had kept Nuna with us, the gases of his decomposition in the strong air of the cabin would have poisoned us all. As it was, with no air to continue the process of decay, he traveled there in space, a few yards away from us, in the same state of preservation as when we put him out. It was impossible to believe he was moving at all—he seemed motionless, just outside the window, staring in at us, as it were, with his glazed jelly-fish eyes.

And so he remained. As our journey neared its end I told myself I would not look through the port-hole to watch the inevitable happen—and yet I knew, in my heart, that I would. When we were within the gravity pull of earth, and were preparing for the landing, with its bout of unconsciousness, I lay on the bed with my head on one side, staring out at the still figure of the little Martian. My heart was beating, I remember, and I trembled.

The end, when it came, was very sudden. And it was —and it is the only word, in spite of all the unpleasant associations of the thing—very beautiful too.

Mac looked at me significantly.

"It's almost time, Steve," he said quietly.

And a moment of two after that, it happened. For a diminutive fraction of a second the figure of Nuna glowed absolutely incandescent—every fiber of his tendrils, his whole outline, burned with unbelievable brilliance against the darkness of space. Only for a flash—and then . . . he was gone! Where he had been, there was nothing.

223

Our last contact with Mars had gone. Perhaps, on earth, some dreamer gazing skywards had seen, that night, a brief trail of fire—a shooting star, as he would think, gone out of his knowledge almost before he had time to register it. . . .

As for us, we remained dazed for a moment or two, looking at each other solemnly. And then the brief unconsciousness came, as I have described it, and when we recovered from that, it was all over. . . .

(*A Note by the Editor of MacFarlane's Papers*. At this point the book sent to me by Stephen MacFarlane comes to an end. There were, in his writing, several disjointed notes that he intended shaping into a closing sequence— I have already referred, earlier in this volume, to the incompleteness of the manuscripts with which I was provided. These notes, unlike his earlier ones, are almost unintelligible—it is quite impossible to reconstruct from them exactly how he proposed to shape his last paragraphs. I have, therefore, not thought it worth while to reprint them here. I leave the end of Chapter XII as above.

One task remains to me, as editor. That is, to explain how the preceding Mss. came into my possession at all —how it came about that I saw this book through the press instead of MacFarlane himself.

This explanation I set forth now in the form of an Epilogue, which you will find on the next page. I apologize for intruding myself on you—as editor, I should, by rights, remain very inconspicuous in the background. But, as I think you will agree, the intrusion is entirely pardonable. The Epilogue is an integral part of the book, if only in the sense that it is an integral part of the story of MacFarlane.—J.K.C.)

AN EPILOGUE, BY JOHN KEIR CROSS

Being the End of the Story of Stephen MacFarlane

ONE day, at my flat in Glasgow, I received a bulky parcel through the post. It contained a pile of manuscripts and two letters. One of the letters was loose on top of the manuscripts, the other was in an envelope marked: *Not to be opened till you have read through the contents of the parcel.*

I glanced first at the loose letter. It was quite short—one page. I recognized the close, cramped hand-writing of my cousin, Stephen MacFarlane. This is what I read:

My dear John,—It is a long time since I have seen you, but you seem, somehow, because of your own literary inclinations, and because of all our deep private association, to be the natural man to turn to in the *impasse* in which I find myself.

You will have read, no doubt, of the extraordinary stir created some months back by the flight to Mars I undertook with my old friend Andrew McGillivray, and the three children, Paul and Jacqueline Adam and Mike Malone. The various papers and magazines have issued articles from time to time (though not much lately, confound them!) describing what we saw on Mars and in space, but so far no really coherent account of the adventure has appeared in print. Attached to this letter you will find the manuscript of a book that should remedy this. It is the story of the whole experience from the beginning to the end, as told from the different points of view of each one of us that underwent it. I want you to read through these papers carefully. When you have done so, *and not before*, open the other letter I have written to you, which I also enclose in this package.

I hope you enjoy the reading. As a literary man, you will at least be amused by some of the charming *gaucheries* in the children's style. Yours ever,—Stephen.

I set the parcel aside, and that evening, when I had finished my day's work, and eaten a meal, sat down to give the book the careful reading my cousin had demanded for it. It was, of course, the book you have just read.

I shall not weary you with a description of my reactions to the extraordinary tale. It will be sufficient to say that as I read, flashes of recognition came into my mind as I encountered some episode or description that had been written up in the Press. I am not a careful reader of the papers, but I did undoubtedly remember the great stir the news of the flight of the *Albatross* had caused—more so than usual because of the part my friend and cousin had played in the adventure. I also remembered that after the flurry of the first few weeks, a note of skepticism had begun to creep into the accounts—leader-writers began to say that it was all very well having a magnificent excuse for not having brought back any proof of the visit, but was it not just possible that it was *only* an excuse? No one had actually seen the *Albatross* land except three very simple-minded old French peasants. It was not beyond the bounds of possibility that the *Albatross* (which was, they had to admit, since it had been examined by trustworthy scientists, a working rocket) had made nothing so spectacular as a flight through space, but had, perhaps, made only a short earth flight from some quiet spot, landing at Azay. Why such a mammoth deception *should* be practiced they had no idea—the incurable urge in some human beings to hoax their fellow men, perhaps (after all, three of the inmates of the rocket had been schoolchildren, who are notoriously given to japes of all sorts—and another passenger had been a professional writer, skilled in the weaving of authentic-sounding romances) . . . at any rate, without casting any real aspersions on the integrity of the people concerned, they took leave to wonder, etc., etc.

As I say, memories of all this came into my head as I read through the book. When I finished it, in the early hours of the morning, there was no doubt in my own mind that the skeptical complaints in the papers had been quite unjustified—no one could, for no seeming reason, have *invented* such a fantastic tale. Why should they?—what gain could possibly accrue to them from doing so? I attributed the remarks of the leader-writers to the insatiable desire of journalists to create a sensation at all costs. The technique seemed quite clear to me: first of all, create a sensation by spreading a story of a flight to Mars, then, when that begins to pall as news, stimulate fresh interest (to say nothing of the circulation of the paper!)

228

by alleging that the whole thing has been a pack of lies—
thus creating a sensation all over again.

I was soon to see that Stephen MacFarlane and Dr.
McGillivray were much more prone to be affected by the
adverse remarks in the Press than I had been. When I
reflect on my cousin's character, I must confess that this
does not surprise me. Let me give you a brief description
of him—it is conceivable that it will interest you, since
you have just finished reading some of his works, and
may, indeed, from time to time, have come across one or
two others of his publications.

He is (perhaps I should say "was," though I am loath
to) a man of middle years, yet with something perpetually young about him. This is all the more surprising when
you reflect that he is, basically, of a melancholy nature:
secretive—as it were, haunted. He is good company, but
you invariably feel that he is only superficially so—all the
time, behind his merriest remark, there lurks this other
sensitive self: a self preoccupied with turning over deep
problems and seeking a solution to them. He believes in
things profoundly and sincerely, and is hurt when people
doubt his beliefs, though he invariably greets their criti-
cisms of him with some disarmingly witty remark. In
short, he is a mixture—what was called, in old German
mythology, a *doppelganger*. As such, an enigma.

This man had proclaimed, in all sincerity, that he had
left the earth and gone to another world. And the world
in which he lived had doubted the genuineness of the
claim. I do not think there is a great reason to be sur-
prised that he took the course of action he has taken.

The Angry Planet

I reproduce now the second letter he wrote to me—the one I opened, according to his instructions, after I had read the pile of manuscripts. This is what it said:

My dear John,—You will by this time have read the manuscripts by myself and my companions setting out our account of our journey to Mars. I was keen for you to do this before hearing what I have to say now, because I believe that anyone who reads the book will reject the accusations against Dr. McGillivray and myself made recently in the papers—and, as you will see, I consider it imperative that you *should* have faith in my integrity before reading any further.

What I want you to do is to take these papers you have read, edit them, and have them published—act, in short, as my literary executor! You will ask why I pass this task to you, when obviously I myself am the man to do it. The reason is very simple. I shall not be here to do it. By the time you read these words, I shall be in outer space—I shall be, my dear John, on *my way back to Mars!* —and for the very good reason, among others, that I prefer an Angry Planet to a Mean, Envious, Uncharitable Planet.

Let me tell you briefly what has happened. I shall be objective—I cannot hope to *explain* my feelings. In any case, one never can explain things—one can only make statements. So I shall, here, content myself with describing the circumstances that have contributed to the formation of my present feelings in my heart.

When we first returned from Mars the world greeted us with acclaim and jubilation—we were heroes, conquerors, and very, very glorious. We were invited to talk at innumerable meetings, we were interviewed, we wrote articles. But gradually a note of doubt crept in. We were accused—we, who had gone through so much!—of deliberate deception. We had no *proof* that we had been to Mars—and therefore, according to the specious arguments of those who are, by a stroke of irony, professional liars themselves, we could not possibly have been to Mars at all!

I have described, in the course of my writings, the character of Dr. McGillivray—a reticent man, interested above all else in his work. You know something of my own personality. You can imagine our feelings, therefore, when we were confronted by this sudden change-round of public opinion—feelings of infinite weariness of spirit and contempt, rather than the more obvious resentment. As for the children, well, as far as this aspect of things is concerned, they hardly matter a great deal. To them, the whole thing was an adventure—it did not have the almost mystic solemnity of occasion it had for us. They are quite happy—they know it happened: they are chagrined, of course, that people do not believe them, but they are young, and look at things objectively. We were concerned with the establishment of scientific truths—not only in having an adventure. Ours is the profounder fate —the fate of Galileo, for example, confronting the Inquisition.

At first, we did not mind the opposition a great deal —it was, in a way, natural to expect it from the popular Press, from a world such as ours with its hideously twisted

231

sense of values. The mob always condemns that which it cannot understand—it is motivated almost entirely by envy: it hates those people who do things that it, in its heart, would like to do, but everlastingly cannot. No, all that was understandable. What galled us was when the scientific world itself began to doubt us.

The trouble began with Kalkenbrenner of Chicago. I have mentioned him in the course of the book—in the introductory chapter, to be precise. He was a rival of Dr. McGillivray's—a man himself profoundly interested in rocket flight. After our return from Mars he came over to see us, to have a look at the *Albatross*. It was obvious from the beginning that he was jealous that Mac had succeeded in solving the problem of inter-stellar flight before he had. He sneered at everything we said. In his heart he believed us, but his pride was so great that he pretended he did not. Where were our proofs? he kept on saying— we had no photographs, no samples, nothing—nothing but an array of plausible excuses.

The snowball grew. Kalkenbrenner, after all, is a man of great reputation and influence. Other scientists associated themselves with him in his decrying of our achievement—men small in spirit but large in numbers, and therefore a force to be reckoned with. Mac was asked to resign from several societies and professional clubs—one by one the scientific journals stopped commissioning articles from him.

All this, you must understand, has come to a head since the book you have just read was written—that is why there is no reference to it all in its pages. The se-

quence of events was this: 1. We returned from Mars.
2. We lectured and were fêted. 3. We went to Pitlochry
for a rest, and wrote the book. At the end of the holiday,
the children went back home, leaving me to put the various manuscripts in order. 4. The rot set in.

And 5—Mac and I decided that we had had enough,
and were going to leave the whole ungrateful crew—were
going to leave them in the most irrevocable way of all:
not by becoming hermits, or anything like that, but by
disappearing from the earth altogether!

That, dear John, is why you are being appointed my
literary executor while I am still alive—an event unparal-
leled, I imagine, in the history of letters.

We made our plans a month ago—secretly: even more
secretly than the last time. On this trip there will be no
stowaways. It was good having the children with us, but
it must be faced—Mars is no place for them.

The day before yesterday we decided the time of our
departure. Yesterday and to-day have been spent in clearing up our affairs. I write this letter to you in the afternoon. When I have finished it, I shall pack up the parcel
and go into Pitlochry to post it. It should reach you to-
morrow, in the midday delivery. By that time we shall
have gone—our time of departure is 10.43 to-morrow
morning!

The *Albatross*, shining and new-looking, after being re-
equipped by Mac, is waiting for us in the enclosure (it
was brought here by road from London shortly after our
return from the first flight). It is our mechanism of escape

—our road to salvation! *Ave atque vale,* Cousin!—hail and farewell!

One word more. I want you personally at least to understand exactly why we are going. First, there is the reason I have mentioned—we are tired and ashamed of being misunderstood. But this does not mean we are not necessarily coming back. If we are spared on this trip, as we were on the last one, we might indeed return—we might even be forced again to return. But this time at least we shall try to remain longer, so that we can do more research—we really hope to try to remain for several years. And when—and if—we do come back, we shall this time bring proof, so that the world may be convinced at last —that, if you like, is our second reason for wanting to make the long, long journey.

But behind and above these, there is a third reason— a more romantic one, perhaps, but to me, even more than to Mac, a potent one. Ever since we came back to earth I have found myself haunted by thoughts of the Beautiful People. Somehow, although we were with them for so short a time, they wormed their way most deeply into my affections. They were so simple, so charming, so infinitely wise in their very *detachment* from things, if you can understand what I mean. And I found myself often, in the night perhaps, growing full of a longing to see them again, so that I might explore them more fully— or, even more simply, so that I might experience again that ineffable sense of benevolence that came merely from being with them. The city we saw, the friends we made—these were destroyed. But there are other cities, and other friends. Malu perhaps escaped that terrible day of the attack and the eruption. Who knows? At any rate, it is in my bones that I must find out.

We may not ever see the Beautiful People—we may be captured and devoured by the Terrible Ones. But we are, on this trip, more equipped to deal with these monsters, at least—it is something that Mac has been working on.

It is all, at any rate, worth taking a chance on. Perhaps some day I shall be able to let you know what develops— what even stranger creatures we may find on that other world across the skies. . . . Perhaps, dear John—perhaps.

Finally, let me say a few words about the manuscript I have asked you to edit and publish. It is, I fear, not quite complete. When the children returned home from their holiday, there were one or two passages I personally had still to do some work on. We knew the shape of the book—that had been very carefully planned from the beginning. I wrote nearly all my own contributions, but just occasionally I left a gap—a passage I wanted to spend some time on, and intended therefore to go back to when I saw the overall design of the volume before me—you, as a writer, will know the way it is. Most of these passages you will be able to tidy over and make coherent— there is only one where there is a serious gap, and that is at the beginning of Chapter V. However, I have no doubt you will contrive something. The end too is rather abrupt and incomplete. I apologize for these flaws—I would have remedied them, but in all the turmoil of this past month, ever since we decided to leave, there has simply not been time.

I may say that I want you to publish the book because, since it has been written, it seems a pity not to do something with it. It might, too, mean a little something financially for the children—I leave you to make arrangements about that. Finally, it just may help to convince people of the truth of our experiences.

Well, John, there it is. I may see you again—I can say no more than that. A flight through space is a dangerous, a terribly dangerous thing. Last time we were lucky—this time we may not be so lucky. And since there in a chance that this is the end of Mac and me, I say a good-bye to you in this letter. I cannot deny that there are many things I regret to be leaving—I regret, almost foremost among them, the end of our friendship. We have been very close to each other—I have always felt, deep in my heart, that you have understood me better than anyone else; and perhaps I can say, without presuming too much, that I have, in my own way, understood you. Sometimes I must have been a torment to you, with those "dark and secret ways" of mine, as you have called them. But withal, there have been the good times, and it is always the good times that matter. I lost my real hold on you when you met A—I always knew that, but somehow I was reluctant to give you up altogether, even though it was only the shell I clung to. Now, at last, I remove myself.

I leave and maybe lose the world—and somehow I count it well lost. I can be assumed dead—and this brings me naturally, by way, as it were, of an epitaph to myself,

to that great passage from our favorite playwright that
we used so often to quote to each other:

> *What do the dead do, uncle? do they eat,*
> *Hear music, go a-hunting, and be merry,*
> *As we that live?*
> >   *No, coz; they sleep.*
> *Lord, Lord, that I were dead!*
> *I have not slept these six nights. . . .*

Good-bye, dear John. Remember me.

STEPHEN.

The morning after reading this letter I rushed straight
to Pitlochry by the first train. There might, I argued, have
been a delay—perhaps MacFarlane and the Doctor had
not left, as they had intended.

But MacFarlane's cottage was empty. I found my way
to the Doctor's laboratory, and it was empty. The big
wooden door of the enclosure at the back of the house
(that enclosure I seemed to know so well from Paul's
description of it in the book)—that door was open; and
through it I saw that the enclosure was empty too. In
the center of it was a long sloping platform of wood, and
that was all.

All I learned in Pitlochry, from the inhabitants, was
that at a quarter to eleven or thereabouts the morning
before, they had heard a loud explosive rushing sound—
"exactly like the noise last summer, when Dr. McGillivray and Mr. MacFarlane and them three children went
missing."

From Mrs. Duthie, MacFarlane's housekeeper, whom

I traced in the town, I got the addresses of the three children. I went to England and called on them—Mike in London, Paul and Jacky in Dorset. They had had, all three of them, letters of farewell from MacFarlane and the Doctor, in which they explained that they were going back to Mars. Mike was disappointed that they had not asked him to go too, or that he had not had a chance to stow away again. As for the others, Paul did not seem to mind, and Jacky was positively relieved that they had not been invited!

The children hardly cared about the lack of belief in the truth of all their experiences. As Mike said: "If they don't believe us, so much the worse for them—that's all I say. Some folk are on our side, and they're the ones that count." And he added, darkly: "We know what we know, that's what! . . ."

As you have seen, I have followed MacFarlane's instructions in the editing and publishing of the book. I was able to fill in the few gaps, knowing his style and working from his copious notes. The serious gap at the beginning of Chapter V I have dealt with as indicated in the separate remarks I have written for it.

The book has taken six months in the printing and binding. In all that time I have looked for a possible return of my friend. There has been no sign. The little red orb of that Angry Planet of his has winked at me inscrutably as I have stared, in the night, into space, wondering and wondering. And that has been all.

The End of the Story

Will he and the Doctor came back?—will they ever come back?

I permit myself, in conclusion, a personal gesture. Because of MacFarlane's farewell to me, in the letter, I say farewell to him across the wide, wide spaces that separate us—just in case he should never return. Farewell, Stephen! —wherever you are, rest in peace. I shall remember, never fear.

And that is the end of the story of Stephen MacFarlane, and the end of this book, THE ANGRY PLANET. Who knows, it may some day have a sequel. For the moment it stands alone—MacFarlane and the Doctor must have taken with them the two long volumes they were working on, as explained in the text, for I have found no trace of them at Pitlochry. Until some other work is forthcoming, then, this remains as the only account of the first great flight of the *Albatross*.

THE END